MIDAS
TOUCH

by frankie j. jones

Bella
BOOKS

Bella Books, Inc
Box 10543
Tallahassee, FL 32302

Printed in the United States of America
First Edition

Editor: Greg Herren
Cover designer: Bonnie Liss (Phoenix Graphics)

ISBN 0-7394-4249-X

For Martha
My fishing partner
Traveling companion
My life
May the rainbows never end

Acknowledgments

I want to thank my partner, Martha Cabrera, for reading the manuscript more times than anyone should ever have to, and for her insight in helping me take my characters where they needed to go. She encouraged to me to keep working, when all I wanted to do was toss the PC out the window.

Thanks to Peggy Herring for her first, second, and yes, even third reading of the manuscript. Peggy, I promise I will not put a single *scream* in my next manuscript.

Thanks to my new editor, Greg Herren. His patience and suggestions pushed me to try a little harder.

Thanks to Kelly Smith for continuing to work 27 hours a day (no that is not a typo) to insure Bella Books remains the first choice in lesbian literature.

CHAPTER ONE

The silver Jag roared off in a blur, leaving Sandra glowering after it. She envisioned the valets joy-riding around Dallas in her car. The unpleasant scenario ended abruptly as a sleek black Mercedes glided into the vacated space and disgorged four laughing women. They had barely stepped away from the vehicle before it, too, zoomed away with another smartly dressed valet at the wheel.

"Nobody gives a damn about anything anymore," Sandra sighed, watching the car's taillights disappear behind a long hedgerow.

Carol dug her nails into Sandra's arm, cutting Sandra's complaints short. "Don't you dare make a scene. Your precious car is perfectly fine."

Sandra watched the four women make their way up the brightly-lit walkway.

Carol tugged at her arm. "Come on. I want to see what Lona Cromwell is wearing. I swear it would not surprise me to find her stark naked. She thrives on shocking the world."

Sandra took a deep breath and gazed at the Cromwell mansion. The three-story, red brick and Texas limestone, transitional Victorian, built by Lona's great-grandfather in 1892, overlooked a spectacular view of the Reunion Tower and downtown Dallas. Three acres of lavish English gardens surrounded the house. Lona employed a staff of four full time gardeners to maintain the gardens. Architecturally, the house was beautiful, but to Sandra, something about it always felt cold and uninviting. She pulled her jacket tighter to ward off the sudden chill creeping over her.

"Stop tugging at your clothes," Carol admonished, swatting Sandra's hands away from her jacket. "You're stretching the material all out of shape." She eyed Sandra's gown with disapproval as she rearranged the jacket. "I wish you would buy yourself some decent clothes. It's not like you can't afford to dress better."

Sandra examined her ensemble. The pale green gown, with spaghetti straps, flowed gracefully from beneath the matching bolero jacket. Beadwork, in a small understated geometric design, embellished the bottom front of the dress and the left front of the jacket. She thought the three-inch heels, with cut-away sides, were especially stunning.

Carol thought differently. "Look at your hair." She began to push Sandra's short hair behind her ears. "I wish you would make an appointment with André. He would work wonders on you."

Carol gathered the shoulders of Sandra's jacket in her hands. "You've lost weight. This jacket is too big on you." She shook her head and released a long-suffering sigh. "You'll never change. You're like a little girl playing dress up."

2

Sandra shrugged the comments off. Carol was right. She would never truly fit in with Carol's world. The designer gown did nothing for her. She was too busy to spend hours shopping or running to hairdressers.

Sandra Tate was a highly successful architect and one of the richest women in Dallas. Her wealth compensated for the fact she was not necessarily pretty. She possessed a rather plain face. Each passing year added more gray to her short, mousy-brown hair. People rarely dwelled on these flaws because Sandra Tate had the Midas Touch. Any project she was involved in was sure to prosper.

She owned Tate Enterprises, a multi-million dollar empire that included among its assets an architectural firm and a large construction company. One of her major accomplishments was the design of a new concept in shopping malls.

Geared to the needs of small towns, the malls blended aesthetically into the site location and reflected local history. She personally negotiated with a major grocery chain and a retail merchandise giant to place stores in each of these malls.

Sandra's community influence and popularity grew in proportion to her wealth. Charity boards vied for her time, and an endorsement from her was a major triumph for any organization. She was one of the most sought after individuals in Dallas. She hated every minute of it.

Another car arrived, snapping Sandra from her musing.

"Carol, why are we attending this party? You despise two-thirds of the women who will be here," Sandra said.

"We've been through this a dozen times. Lona Cromwell's party is *the* social event of the year. Anyone who is anyone will be here tonight," Carol said. "Besides, we have to make an appearance. You've not attended anything with me in ages and people are starting to talk." She stopped short and drew her lips into a defiant pout.

Sandra gazed down at her. Lona Cromwell's yearly extravaganza of Who's Who was the sort of event Carol lived for.

Tonight was important to her. Glancing down at her ensemble, Sandra felt a pang of guilt. For Carol's sake, she should try harder to fit into the role expected of her.

Sandra looked at Carol, trying to see her as a stranger would.

Carol Grant was a beautiful woman. She religiously attended daily aerobic sessions to keep her forty-one-year-old body slim and well-toned. Weekly tanning appointments kept Carol's skin perfectly bronzed year round. Her luxurious blond hair, pulled into a French braid, showed no telltale signs of aging. Only a sprinkling of fine lines beginning to etch their way into the corners of her gray eyes hinted at her actual age. Unfortunately, Carol's beauty was skin deep.

During the last few months, Sandra often found herself wondering why she had fallen in love with Carol eight years ago. Why had she not seen how petty and manipulative Carol could be? She pushed the thoughts away. It was not fair to blame everything on Carol.

From their first date, Sandra had conceded to Carol's every whim. Recently, something changed within Sandra. She grew weary of the constant giving. She tried to determine what was different, but was unable to pinpoint the change. After all, Carol was the same as she had been since birth: a spoiled little girl accustomed to receiving everything she wanted.

Carol tugged at Sandra's arm. Sandra pushed away her doubts and pasted on a smile. She had agreed to come tonight. She could at least be civilized and make the best of it.

"I'm sorry. I'm being intolerable," Sandra apologized and took Carol's arm. "I promise not to spoil your evening."

Carol flashed her a lazy, seductive smile that brought back memories of the woman Sandra had fallen in love with. The moment should have reassured her, but now it merely signaled an end to their current argument.

4

They strolled up the broad limestone walkway and through one of the three grand arches gracing the front of the mansion.

A string quartet, unobtrusively tucked behind a screen laced with rare tropical flowers, performed a soothing melody that followed them as they crossed a wide porch and entered the house.

Inside, a small army of staff greeted them and waited to take their jackets. Sandra stood by as Carol slipped out of her gorgeous black silk, sequined and beaded evening jacket. Beneath it, Carol wore an elegant black gown with a plunging v-shaped neckline. A delicate over-the-shoulders y-shaped back strap held the gown up, leaving her well-toned back exposed. Her only jewelry was a small diamond pendant suspended on a thin gold chain.

A young woman from the staff stepped forward help Sandra with her jacket, but Sandra opted to keep it. She was cold and the thought of nothing but the thin spaghetti straps left to warm her shoulders only served to make her colder. She could feel Carol's disapproving frown, but ignored her.

The young woman who offered to help Sandra with her jacket escorted them up a long circular stairwell.

Sandra looked over the rail into the immense foyer below. The black and white Italian marble floor reflected hundreds of pinpoints of rainbow hues cast from the massive chandelier. Wood moldings, displaying the handiwork of a master carver, separated the cream-colored walls from the pristine white ceiling.

They climbed to the ballroom on the third floor, and here, Sandra again experienced the shock she felt every time she saw the modern changes. Lona had replaced the original satin wallpaper with custom-made black leather panels lining the high walls from floor-to-ceiling. Inserted at three feet intervals were floor to ceiling silver framed mirrors. The marble floor glistened like black onyx. Strobe lights placed discreetly around the room bounced off the floor and mirrors, filling the space with shimmering waves of light.

The only windows were those in the French doors leading to a magnificent balcony. Also leading from the room was the doorway where Sandra and Carol stood, and a third door opening into a long hallway. The latter door led to an enormous restroom better suited to a stadium than a private home. A long narrow kitchen, used by the catering staff, was located across from the restroom.

Numerous sitting areas were scattered around the room. Two long mahogany bars ran across either side. Dozens of tuxedoed waitstaff glided about the already crowded room offering trays laden with exotic drinks and food.

A shiver of revulsion ran down Sandra's back as she stepped into Lona Cromwell's ballroom. The room left Sandra feeling cold and depressed. What kind of mind conceived such décor?

Sandra focused on the vibrant hues of the women's gowns deriving a small sense of warmth from them. The two hundred or so women invited tonight were the créme-de-la-créme of Dallas' lesbian society. They held positions ranging from fashion model to national-level political seats.

In her element, Carol transformed into a smiling, bubbling socialite. Anyone seeing the long, endearing glances she directed to her lover, Sandra Tate, would assume theirs was the perfect relationship.

As they stepped into the room, Lona Cromwell's tall, willowy frame floated toward them. Sandra felt an almost irresistible urge to lift the train of Lona's black silk gown to see if her feet ever touched the floor. She shook off the thought, reminding herself to behave.

Lona bent to embrace Carol's petite five-foot-three body. Listening to their exclamations, a stranger might think they were best friends, when in reality they barely tolerated each other. Their social circle required they remain civil.

6

Lona was a classic beauty and a product of old Texas money. Her family's roots went back to Stephen F. Austin's original settlers. The Cromwell name was as familiar in the oil fields as it was in the hallways of the Capitol building in Austin. Lona held degrees in corporate law and chemical engineering, but never used either of them. She held token positions on the board of directors of two major corporations in which her father had gained a controlling interest.

She spent her time flying off to one tropical paradise or another, always in the company of at least one beautiful woman. It was seldom the same woman.

Lona turned to Sandra. "I'm so glad you came tonight. You're always missing my little affairs." She brushed a kiss on Sandra's lips as silky strands of her long, black hair trailed along Sandra's arm.

"Sandra insists she has to work twenty hours a day or the day is wasted," Carol said with a short laugh.

Sandra heard the harsh edge in Carol's laughter.

"You should be grateful she cares enough to work so hard for you," Lona admonished, never taking her eyes from Sandra.

Seeing the flash of anger in Carol's eyes, Sandra stepped forward and took her arm. "We were on our way to get something to drink," Sandra said.

A new group of guests swept in on a wave of noisy laughter. Sandra used the distraction to whisk Carol away. At the bar, she ordered Carol a scotch, and a club soda for herself. She seldom drank alcohol, not liking the loss of control it produced.

Sandra tried to focus her attention on the activities around her. The waitstaff moved smoothly among the milling guests with trays weighed down with beluga caviar and a variety of other delicacies. In the far corner, an all-woman band performed an old Stevie Nicks song. Sandra became so engrossed in the music, she flinched when a husky voice whispered in her ear.

7

"There you are."

Before she could respond, tentacle-like arms encircled her waist.

A flicker of irritation flashed in Carol's eyes. Sandra knew she would hear about this later.

"Hello, Janice," Sandra replied, maneuvering away from the clinging arms before turning to kiss the proffered cheek.

Janice Knight was one of the hottest models in New York. Even without heels, the African American goddess towered over most of the women in the room.

Sandra met Janice the previous year at a fund-raiser for the battered women's shelter. Before the benefit ended, Janice made it quite clear to Sandra she was available for anything, any time Sandra chose to call. Sandra moved farther back as Carol stepped between them.

"Janice darling, you're looking so much better," Carol oozed.

Janice's startling blue, contact-enhanced eyes narrowed at the mention of her recent near disaster. In the middle of a photography session for a new cosmetic line, her face began to swell in frightening proportions. The allergic reaction left her skin blotched and chafed for several days. Fortunately, the reaction caused no lasting damage. Rumors suggested the pending lawsuit would be more lucrative than the original seven-figure contract.

"Carol, why don't you drop by the studio next week?" Janice said as a small smile curled her lip. "Perhaps one of the consultants can help you with some of your skin problems."

Carol's back stiffened as she inhaled sharply. Deciding the two had drawn enough blood for one night, Sandra again took Carol firmly by the arm. "Why don't we go say hello to Joan and Sarah? We'll catch you later, Janice."

"Why don't you come back alone?" Janice whispered as Sandra brushed past her.

"Did you hear what she said to me?" Carol wailed when

8

they were out of earshot. "And did you see that horrid turquoise rag she was wearing?"

Sandra glanced at Janice's gown. She would never consider herself an expert on fashion, but even she recognized a Versace. Discretion kept Sandra from disagreeing with Carol, but she thought the gown looked stunning on the pencil-thin model.

"She's jealous," Sandra lied to reassure Carol.

"What did she say to you?" Carol demanded as one hand flew to her hip.

Exhaustion settled over Sandra like a shroud. Carol's jealousy was more than she could handle right now.

"She's trying to take you away from me," Carol whined, glaring across the room at Janice. With a defiant toss of her head, she drained her scotch and whirled to confront Sandra.

"Have you been seeing her? Is she the reason you're never home?"

Sandra felt her self-control slipping. She had been working twelve and fourteen hour days for the past two weeks. Operating a business the size of Tate Enterprises required more work than Carol could ever imagine.

"When do you think I have time to see anyone?" she whispered, trying to curb her growing irritation.

"You leave at dawn and don't come home until midnight." The music ended abruptly and Carol's comment was loud enough to attract the attention of a group of women. They stopped their conversation to stare, eagerly awaiting the ensuing drama.

To their disappointment, Sandra led Carol onto the balcony. The night air was growing colder, but neither seemed to notice.

"Carol, I don't intend to go into this again. Why do you always do this?"

"I don't know what you're talking about," Carol insisted as she turned away from Sandra and stared out over the city.

"You know exactly what I mean. You insist we come to

9

these things and then you make a big scene the first time some woman looks at me."

"You flirt with other women," Carol sniffed.

"No, Carol. Other women flirt with me," Sandra replied. "I am so tired of your never-ending accusations. I've done nothing to justify your jealousy, but you never seem to understand. You knew how it would be from the beginning. It's the money. That's all they're interested in." *Just like you*, she finished silently. "If I worked at Wal-Mart they wouldn't give me a second glance." Sandra flung her arms in frustration, sending a splash of club soda over her hand. "Damn!" She set the glass on a table and wiped her hand with a napkin.

"You don't love me anymore," Carol said, her sniffs growing louder.

"Please, don't start. I'm tired and . . ."

Carol whirled to face her. "You're always tired. If any of those bitches in there knew what a lousy lover you are, they wouldn't be so hot for you!" Without waiting for Sandra's reply, Carol stormed across the balcony and disappeared inside.

Stunned, Sandra turned her attention to the city lights. A remnant of the old thrill ran through her as she sighted one of her designs, the Strauss Building, her first major project in Dallas. She gazed at the structure as a mother would a child. It had been a long, hard process, but she had been involved in every step of its creation. She recalled the joy she once felt in designing a new building. How she had thrived on creating beautiful buildings that would survive the rigors of time. At some point in the last few years, her work stopped providing the same thrill. When had it all changed? When had she lost her enthusiasm for her work? All she wanted was . . . *was what*, she wondered? What did she want?

Exhausted, she leaned her back against the cold stone wall for support. The French doors swung open and Sandra groaned as Lona Cromwell stepped out. Too late, she realized she should have followed Carol back inside. If success had taught her anything, it was that money was the world's most powerful aphrodisiac.

"Are you okay?" Lona asked. She stopped short of actually touching Sandra.

Sandra tried to move away, but the corner of the balcony trapped her.

"I'm fine," she said. "I've been working too hard." She attempted to edge past, but Lona placed her hand on the wall blocking her way.

"You need a woman who understands you," Lona whispered, pressing her body against Sandra. She ran her hand along Sandra's cheek. "I know what you need. I could make you happy."

Sandra pushed Lona away. "What I need is none of your concern." She sidestepped Lona and returned to the party.

The room was much more crowded than it had been before she stepped outside. After the bracing cold of the balcony the room felt overheated. Sandra searched for Carol in the swarm of over-dressed women. She heard Carol's laughter from across the crowded room. How odd it was to hear Carol laugh. She seldom laughed anymore. As Sandra drew closer, she saw Carol talking to a blonde who looked familiar.

The band struck up a rousing rendition of "Proud Mary" and Sandra groaned. *Did every band in the world know that song?* Women were beginning to dance. A short heavy-set woman Sandra recognized as a district judge, bumped into her. Sandra felt the judge's drink hit her arm and looked down in time to see a dark, sticky stain begin to spread across the front of her gown. The woman was apologizing, but Sandra waved her off and continued to make her way toward Carol. The heat and noise pressed down on Sandra. She tried to focus on a single individual or conversation, but the multitude of smells from the food, alcohol, and dozens of different perfumes wrapped around her like sheets of cellophane wrap. She struggled to keep her breathing regular as the tightness in her chest grew. The short, sharp pains plaguing her during the past week came back. There was not enough oxygen in the room. She turned trying to make her way back to the balcony, but Lona stood at the door waiting for her. Sandra stumbled toward the kitchen. With these women, the kitchen would be the safest room in which to hide. She was nearing her sanctuary when she spied Janice cutting her off. Sandra whirled around and pushed her way back across the floor. Carol was still talking to the blonde, but Sandra no longer cared about protocol. The only thing important was escaping the crush of the room.

"Let's go," she insisted, taking Carol's arm.

Carol's mouth pulled into a grim line. "I'm not ready to go."

The noise level continued to grow around Sandra. The bass guitar's pounding beat went straight to Sandra's brain. She tried to block the guitar out. A smirk played across the blonde's lips as she began to tap her nails against her glass. The sound grated in Sandra's ears.

"Carol, I really need to leave," Sandra urged, looking desperately around the room. There was not enough air to breathe, and the room was closing in. The mirrors began playing tricks on her. She was reminded her of the House of Mirrors she and her dad had gone through when she was nine. The grossly distorted images cast by the mirrors had rendered the young Sandra immobile. Her father had to carry her from the building.

She was feeling the same overwhelming sense of confusion. Everywhere she looked, she found a reflection of herself staring back. Voices thundered in her ears. The air filled with swirling red dots. The pain in her chest grew. Her heartbeat accelerated until she was certain it would burst through her chest onto the blonde's immaculate white gown. She had to escape. A blur of surprised, angry faces greeted her as she shoved her way to the door. She heard Lona calling her name, but nothing was going to stop her from getting out. She pushed through a crowd standing in the doorway and made her escape into the hall. Lona called her from the doorway and Sandra ran. She raced down the staircase, oblivious to the startled faces of the women coming up. She heard people calling her name, but it only served to make her run faster. As she approached the first landing, her ankle turned. The heel broke. A sharp stab of pain sliced through her ankle. She was falling. The sensation seemed to last an inordinately long time. She slammed against the wooden railing. Sandra clutched at the cold railing and regained her balance. She rotated her throbbing ankle until the pain began to subside. The only real damage seemed to be her shoe. The broken heel rested against the bottom stair step. Brand new shoes ruined because of her carelessness. Growling in frustration, she ripped the shoe from her foot and flung it against the wall.

A young woman in a black tuxedo appeared on the stairs in front of her. "Ma'am, let me help you." She reached for Sandra's arm.

Sandra pushed her aside and rushed down the stairs. The remaining heel made it impossible to run. She kicked it off and ran barefooted. As she burst off the stairs, she came face-to-face with the startled staff at the doorway. Someone reached out to her. She slapped his hand aside and rushed out the door, onto the brightly illuminated porch. A group of surprised valets sprang to life as she charged out.

"The silver Jag," she shouted to the nearest valet.

"Which silver Jag?" he queried, looking at her with both confusion and suspicion.

Sandra started to yell at him when she heard Carol's voice calling her name.

The hell with it, she decided. *Carol can drive herself home.* Sandra turned away from the valets and sprinted down the walkway, across the street, and into the safety of darkness.

Several minutes later, still moving in an awkward shuffling run, she crossed a road and staggered into a park. The streetlights grew farther apart as she ran deeper into the park. Darkness closed around her like a protective cloak. She should go back to the party and apologize for her rudeness, but she was unable to stop.

Sandra moved deeper into the park, the night as dark as her mood. A sprinkler system installed along the sidewalk hissed and soaked the nearby ground. She continued to run, until she smashed into a tree and fell. The dampness from the wet grass soaked through her thin gown. Unable to manage anything other than short hard gasps, she was incapable of inhaling enough oxygen. She wondered if she was dying of a heart attack and tried to fight off the numbness engulfing her. She was not ready to die. So many new experiences awaited her. Her last conscious thought was that she never accomplished the one thing she most wanted in life. She wanted to know her mother.

Birds sang overhead as weak rays of light poked their way through the treetops. Sandra's body ached from lying on the cold, damp ground. Her face burned with shame as the events of the previous night came back to her. How could she have lost control? Never in her life had she let her emotions get so out of hand. As realization of her current situation came to her, fear mobilized her frozen limbs. She was alone in the middle of a park. She needed to leave before someone found her. A thousand scenarios filled her head. None of them appealed to her.

She pushed herself up and took a tentative step. The ankle she twisted coming down the stairs was tender, but nothing seemed to be broken. Her bare feet were bruised and sore. Dried blood caked her left elbow, which protruded through a rip in her jacket. She limped to a bench and tried to get her bearings. She was positive she was still near Lona's house.

How was she going to get home? There was no way she could go back and face Lona. Carol would have driven the car home. Would anyone be looking for her? She cringed at the thought of her photo appearing on the front page of the newspaper. The headline would scream: prominent architect goes berserk and flees lesbian party. She clutched her head in her hands, thanking God the police required a twenty-four hour waiting period before a person could be declared missing. At least, she would avoid that embarrassment.

She did a quick perusal of her appearance. Jagged runs in her stockings spread like spider webs about her legs. Her gown, covered with dirt and grass stains, was beyond repair. The original mid-calf side slit now extended all the way to her hip. The jacket had a hole in the elbow. A button dangled on a shred of torn fabric. Given the current condition of the jacket, Carol's concerns of Sandra stretching the material out of shape were now laughable.

She ran icy hands across her head and encountered a tangled mess of leaves and twigs. Using her fingers, she tried to comb the short brown strands into some semblance of order.

She winced as her palm brushed over a knot above her left eye. That must have happened when she collided with the tree.

What possessed her to go tearing out of Lona's like a crazy woman? When had her life gotten so out of control? A cry of frustrated exhaustion tore from her throat. She tucked her cold hands under her arms and forced herself to calm down. The right planning and determination could put her back on track. The most obvious change needed was to cut back on her hours and stop working so hard. She would schedule a few days off. She and Carol could take a vacation.

A mental image of her calendar for the next several weeks popped into her head, and she reluctantly pushed the vacation idea away. There were too many things going on. It would be impossible for her to leave. She would simply have to get control over her emotions. *I'm probably going through meno-*

pause, she rationalized. Thirty-seven was young, but anything was possible. Maybe it was nothing more than a hormone imbalance. *Maybe, maybe, maybe*, she mumbled to herself.

She took a deep breath and tried to reassure herself. *I'm just tired and under a lot of stress. It's time I stopped trying to do everything on my own. I'll let someone help me. When I get home, we can talk this out, and we will start spending more time together. I'll start leaving the office earlier*, she promised the cold, gray dawn.

A violent chill ripped through her, prodding her to get out of the park before she caught pneumonia, or worse, someone recognized her. Hobbling on her sore feet, she located a phone booth at the edge of the park. With frozen fingers she punched in the long string of memorized numbers from her calling card. There was only one person she felt she could count on — Laura Mendoza.

She and Laura had met during their freshman year at college. They were working in a large Mexican restaurant. Laura was working to help pay her way through college, while Sandra was there on a full scholarship and working for spending money. They became best friends. The resulting friendship endured through the years.

Laura's sleepy voice cut into Sandra's reverie.

"Laur..ra," Sandra's teeth chattered loudly.

"Hello?"

"Laura, it's . . . San . . . dra."

"I can't understand you. Sandra? Is that you?"

"Laura, I need help. Can you come and get me?"

"Where are you? Are you okay?"

"I'm fine." Sandra looked down at her ruined clothes. "I'm near the corner of Medford and Lane, by the park." A chill ripped through her causing her to fumble the telephone. Grabbing it up she continued. "Could you bring a coat and some shoes, please?"

"Coat? Shoes? My God! Sandra, what's wrong? Are you hurt?"

"I'll explain later. Just hurry please."

Luckily, not many people were out this early on a Sunday morning. Sandra moved back farther into the trees where she would be concealed from the casual passerby, but could still watch for Laura. She sat down and leaned against a tree wrapping her arms around her body, knowing it would take Laura at least an hour to reach her.

Forty-five minutes later, she spotted Laura's brand new canary yellow Volkswagen Beetle running a red light and streaking toward the park.

Watching the car race down the road, Sandra realized how much Laura and her car had in common. Both were small but strong and dependable. The little car was just as feisty as its owner.

Sandra stumbled to her feet, ran out, and waved her hands. The Volkswagen skidded to a halt. As she approached the vehicle, Sandra saw the shocked look on Laura's face.

Sandra opened the door to the passenger side after Laura leaned over to unlock it. A blast of delicious warm air engulfed Sandra as she scrambled into the vehicle.

"Christ, Sandra. What happened?"

"Coat." Sandra's teeth chattered unmercifully. She had never been so cold in her life. Laura grabbed a coat from the back seat and helped Sandra struggle into it.

"Are your hurt?" Laura asked, staring at Sandra's torn clothing and shoeless feet. "I'm going to drive you to a hospital," she insisted.

"No! I'm not hurt. Just a little worse for wear."

"Your feet?"

"They're all right. They look worse than they are. Did you bring shoes?"

Again, Laura leaned over into the back seat and retrieved a pair of fuzzy house shoes.

"They are probably a couple of sizes too small, but I thought you could just slip your toes into them," Laura said.

Sandra wiggled her toes into the warm fuzzy slippers. Nothing had ever felt so good on her feet. Shivering, she pulled the coat tighter around her. She felt foolish. How could she explain her bizarre exit from the party? She had no idea what sparked her panic and caused her to flee. "I'm freezing," she said weakly.

Laura switched the heater fan on high.

"Are you sure you don't want to go to a hospital?"

"Yes, I'm sure."

Laura looked unconvinced, but conceded. "Then I'll drive you home."

"No! I'm not ready to face Carol."

Laura hesitated before asking. "Is there somewhere you want to go?"

Sandra turned to stare out the window. "There's no place to go," she replied softly.

"As long as I'm here, you'll always have a place." Laura reached across the seat and gently squeezed Sandra's hand.

CHAPTER TWO

An hour later they walked into Laura's small cottage. Sandra let the calming effect of its cheerful colors and homey atmosphere wash over her. The cottage contrasted drastically with Sandra's penthouse, which Carol had insisted on having decorated by Marvin Dolman, the current guru of interior design. The result was a red velvet and chrome monstrosity Sandra secretly thought of as Whorehouse ala Chez. Of course, Carol loved it. Sandra tolerated it for Carol's sake. She was rarely there anyway.

Laura's warm brown eyes studied Sandra. "You look exhausted. I'm going to run you a hot bath. While you're relaxing, I'll find you something to wear. Then we can eat and talk."

After starting the bath water, Laura removed her coat and hung it on the back of a kitchen chair. She was still wearing her yellow and white checkered pajama top tucked into her jeans. Sensing Sandra's stare, Laura glanced at the top and shrugged.

"What can I say? You scared the shit out of me."

Touched by Laura's concern for her, Sandra swallowed the lump in her throat.

"Would you like to call Carol, to let her know where you are?"

"No." Telling Carol she was at Laura's cottage would only make the situation worse. Carol was unreasonably jealous of Laura and Sandra's friendship.

Laura looked as though she wanted to say more, but instead shook her head and started down the hallway. "Come on. Hop into the tub before you catch pneumonia."

"You don't catch pneumonia from getting chilled."

"Oh yeah. Well, you explain that to my *abuela* Mendoza. Now, get in the tub. There's some first aid supplies in the cabinet if you want to take care of that." She pointed to the cut over Sandra's eye.

Sandra entered the sunny yellow kitchen wearing a black with white trim, fleece-lined, jogging suit two inches too short and the blue fuzzy house slippers. Greeted by the sweet smell of something baking and fresh coffee, she took a deep breath. Some of the tension eased from her body.

Laura had traded her flannel pajama top for a creamy white pullover that complimented her bronze skin.

"If the fashion police could only see you now," Laura teased as she tossed her waist-length ponytail over her shoulder.

"There's already enough for everyone to gossip about. What I'm wearing won't even matter."

Laura pulled a pan of muffins from the oven. She placed two on a plate in front of Sandra. "Sit down. Try these cranberry and apple muffins. It's a new recipe, so tell me what you think." Laura wrote cookbooks and acted as a menu advisor for one of the largest restaurants in Dallas.

Sandra pulled a muffin apart, inhaling the fragrant steam before taking a bite. She closed her eyes in appreciation as the delicious morsel melted in her mouth. "Better than sex," she moaned as she swallowed.

Laura sat a cup of coffee in front of her. "My dear woman, thank you for the compliment, but if you truly believe that, you're doing something wrong."

Sandra gave a sour laugh and sipped her coffee.

"I'm sorry," Laura said, reaching for her hand. "Tell me what's going on."

"I'm not sure I know myself," Sandra admitted, pinching off another piece of muffin. It no longer tasted as wonderful as it had.

"Talk to me," Laura coaxed.

"Nothing feels right anymore. I spend my days running from one meeting to the next. In between meetings, I'm on the telephone setting up more meetings. I can't remember the last time I actually designed a building. My personal life is non-existent." Her voice rose. She took a deep breath and shoved the plate aside.

Laura pushed it back toward her. "Eat," she commanded. "You're skin and bones." She waited until Sandra began to nibble again. "It sounds like you need a vacation."

Sandra snorted. "I don't have time to scratch my butt. How am I supposed to take a vacation?"

"I haven't heard that awful expression since we were in college," Laura said, walking to the counter with their coffee cups and refilling them. "You're the boss," she said, placing a cup back in front of Sandra. "You could get away if you truly wanted to."

Sandra heard the added emphasis to the latter part of

Laura's statement and started to protest, but a small nagging voice stopped her. Laura was right. There were plenty of people at Tate Enterprises who could carry the workload while she was gone. Why was she hesitating? Frustrated, she ran her hands over her face. "That's part of the problem. I don't know what I want."

"Have you talked to Carol?"

Sandra stood abruptly and began to pace. She vaguely noticed the worn red-and-white rag rugs lying before the sink and beneath the antique, unfinished walnut table. The scratches and stains on the table's top read like a hieroglyphic testament of its decades of use.

Glass-fronted cabinets revealed a treasure-trove of mismatched dishes gathered from the innumerable garage sales and flea markets Laura haunted. Nothing matched, yet everything fit together with a sense of completeness Sandra could not explain. There was a serenity here Sandra found nowhere else. After several circuits around the small kitchen, she sat down.

"I feel like my whole life is one big screwed up jumble. Nothing makes sense. I'm not happy at work. I'm not happy at home." She stopped, surprised by her outburst.

"You're doing good. Don't clam up," Laura said, squeezing her hand.

"You're the only person I've ever been able to talk to," Sandra acknowledged, recalling the long nights, starting in college, when she and Laura hashed over their turbulent love lives, or in Sandra's case, the lack of one. After college, their continuing sessions helped work through Laura's failed marriage, the death of Sandra's father, and the ups and downs of their careers. Sandra withdrew her hand and rubbed her eyes. She was so tired.

"What's going on with Carol?" Laura asked with her usual bluntness.

Sandra shrugged. "I don't know. There doesn't seem to be anything left between us except arguing. I can't do anything right where she's concerned. I'm never home. I can't manage to get away when she needs me for something. I embarrass her in front of her friends."

"I'm hearing a lot of *I's* in this conversation. It couldn't be the old tendency you have of trying to carry the weight of the world on those scrawny shoulders of yours, could it?"

Sandra stood up angrily. "I thought we could talk."

Laura's eyebrows knitted together. "We can, as long as we're honest with each other." She pushed her cup away. "Let's start over. What happened last night? Why were you in the park at dawn this morning looking like the loser in a barroom brawl?"

Sandra sat down and slowly revealed the events of the previous evening.

"This is your need to control thing, isn't it?" Laura asked when Sandra fell silent.

"I know you don't understand," Sandra said, "but to me it's important. It's who I am."

Laura frowned. "Haven't you ever just completely let go? No restraints. No worries about what someone else is going to think?"

Sandra looked down at her hands. She began to twist the ring on her finger. The wide gold band, with its intricate black onyx and pearl pattern, was the only material possession she truly cherished.

"What about when you're making love?" Laura asked.

Sandra felt her face turning scarlet. She could not remember the last time she had made love to Carol. It had been almost seven years since she touched Carol. The less than desirable first year had been their best. Even with her lack of experience, she knew something was not right. Early in the relationship, she discovered Carol hated sex. The few times Carol allowed Sandra to make love to her ended with Carol criticizing Sandra's inexperience. Daunted by her inadequacies, Sandra finally stopped touching Carol altogether.

With no prior relationship to base her ability on, Sandra

assumed the problem was her lack of experience. Occasionally, she wondered if there was something more, another reason for Carol's rejection. She once suggested to Carol that maybe their problems in the bedroom stemmed from something other than just her lack of experience. After all, Carol's refusal to allow Sandra to touch her was strange. The mere mention their problems might also include Carol sent her into a rage.

"What could you possibly know about making love?" Carol demanded. "For all your money, Sandra Tate, you're still no more refined than common trailer trash."

The jab cut deep, as Carol knew it would. No matter how much money she made, the number of accolades she received, or how many magazine articles praised her talents, deep down, Sandra Tate was still the little girl who lived in a trailer court. The little girl who raced home from school to clean the trailer and have dinner on the table for her father when he came home. He was the only family she knew, and she'd loved him dearly. She grew up believing it was her responsibility to care for him since her mother abandoned them when Sandra was four. In her heart, Sandra knew she was the reason her mother left. She must have been, because everything had been fine between her parents before she was born.

Sandra's father worked odd jobs, and was constantly hooking up the tiny trailer they called home to relocate to a new city in search of better paying work.

Sandra learned to appreciate the frequent moves. They kept her from having to deal with making friends and explaining why her mother never came to school with cookies and treats on party days.

Their final move to Dallas occurred when Sandra was a senior in high school. This move would eventually turn her life around.

With little spare money for the frivolities enjoyed by other kids, Sandra devised ways to amuse herself. One of her ongoing pastimes was planning the dream home she and her dad would have someday. As she grew older, she accepted the reality that the house would never exist, but continued to dream and sketch. By the time they settled in Dallas, she possessed a battered boot box full of adaptations and additions to the plans.

Fate took a hand in Sandra's life when she enrolled in a home-making course. The instructor, Ms. Angelo, a short, olive-skinned woman who Sandra fell in love with, believed in pushing her students to go beyond the normal cooking and sewing requirements the class normally required. Her major project for the term was to challenge her students to create the house they would someday like to live in. They were to plan and decorate the design. It could be drawn or constructed from the materials on hand. The project was due before Christmas break.

Excited by the project, Sandra allowed herself free rein, knowing this would be as close as she would ever come to building her dream home. She also wanted to show Ms. Angelo she could meet her challenge.

Having lived in what was basically a travel trailer, Sandra's ideas were free of conventional architectural constraints. She constructed a wide, two-story home with a porch spanning the width of the front. Inside, she designed rooms with open seating areas. Many of the rooms displayed unique and slightly hidden alcoves. Each alcove contained a window, which filled the area with sunlight and allowed an unobstructed view of one of the many scenic landscapes she patiently created from twigs and construction paper. She used clever closets to provide an abundance of storage space; something there was never enough of in the small trailer.

Sandra spent two weeks working on the spacious kitchen. She craved sunlight and color, so in addition to the hot house window above the kitchen sink, which she filled with miniature plants, she used thin glass slides to represent a bay window beside the breakfast nook. A row of small, colorful, plastic squares replicated stained glass and ran the length of the outer wall, just below the ceiling. When light struck the model, the kitchen glowed with rainbow hues.

Although she finished the project several days before its due date, Sandra held off turning it in. Every day after school she would sit by the model and dream about someday living in this house. At the last possible hour, she carried the model to the home-making room and gently placed it among the other models.

On her return after Christmas, Sandra found a note on her locker summoning her to report to Ms. Dysan, the student guidance counselor. This was not a new experience for her. The years of moving from school to school often left her re-assuring some adult she was well-adjusted and doing fine. On more than one occasion, they moved so often her school records were lost at some distant location behind her.

During her first and second grade years, she took numerous notes home to her dad requesting her birth cer-tificate. He would read the notes and sigh. A few days later, Sandra would arrive home to find the trailer hitched to the old truck and they would move on to a new town.

Sandra would have a few weeks of peace before the notes began again at the new location. By the third grade, her re-cords were so jumbled no one cared anymore.

Sandra's heart raced when she entered the office and found Ms. Dysan was not alone. Ms. Angelo was there and Sandra's model sat on Ms. Dysan's desk. She experienced a sense of dread. There must be something wrong with her project.

Ms. Dysan smiled and motioned to a chair in front of her desk. "Come in, Sandra. Have a seat. We want to talk to you about your project."

From her chair, Sandra studied the slightly overweight woman, whose short, curly hair framed a face suggesting a no-nonsense attitude.

"Is something wrong?"

"Quite the contrary," Ms. Angelo assured her and gave Sandra a smile that set Sandra's heart pounding. "I'd love to have a sitting room like this."

You can have it, Sandra's heart pledged as Ms. Angelo's fingertips caressed the top of the model. Sandra burned to have them touch her with such loving tenderness.

Ms. Dysan stood and approached the model. "I've never seen such an original plan. What does your father do?"

"My father?" She was having trouble concentrating with Ms. Angelo standing so close. Sandra could smell her perfume. She focused her attention on the floor to keep from staring at Ms. Angelo.

"Yes," Ms. Dysan said, walking around the table where the model sat. "The clever closets and the way these areas are separated, yet part of the room." She pointed to the alcoves. "He must have put a lot of work into this."

Sandra raised her eyes to find both women watching her. They thought her father built her model. There was an instant stiffening of her back and her chin came up.

"My father had nothing to do with it. I did the work myself."

"You did all of this by yourself?" Ms. Dysan asked. "No one helped even a little?" she persisted as a look passed between the two women.

"I didn't need anyone's help," Sandra answered coldly. Why was Ms. Angelo looking at Ms. Dysan as though they shared a secret? They exchanged another glance as Ms. Dysan returned to her desk. Ms. Angelo moved to stand by her. Sandra wanted Ms. Angelo to stand closer to her, to move away from Ms. Dysan who doubted Sandra's honesty.

Ms. Angelo placed her hands in her jacket pockets and leaned onto Ms. Dysan's desk. "How did you know to do this? You never asked me for any help."

"I just knew," Sandra said and shrugged. How could she

explain the finished product was already in her head? All she did was copy it onto the paper.

Ms. Dysan rose and walked to Sandra, handing her a pencil and a pad. "Sandra, if I came to you and said, design me a four bedroom, two bath English Tudor, with a two car garage. How would you design it?"

"Nancy," Ms. Angelo said, so softly it hurt Sandra to listen.

Why did she call this woman by her first name? Sandra wondered. Ms. Dysan gave Ms. Angelo a look and actually patted her hand.

"I wouldn't," Sandra blurted, determined not to let her anger show. People could not hurt you, unless you cared.

"Why not?" Ms. Dysan asked, as she arched a perfect eyebrow.

"Because I don't know what an English Tudor looks like."

Ms. Angelo dropped her head quickly, but not before Sandra saw her smile. A wave of warmth rushed over her.

"I see," Ms. Dysan said, with a slight smile. "Then how did you design this model?"

Sandra thought about it for a moment. "I just copied it from my head."

Ms. Dysan tipped her head to one side and stared at Sandra. "So you've seen it somewhere in a magazine or something?" Ms. Dysan persisted.

"No."

"Sandra," Ms. Angelo said, her dark brown eyes mesmerizing Sandra. "I have a Boston Terrier and two cats. I love to read and listen to music. I hate to cook and have little use for a kitchen. I'm a homebody. When I entertain, I prefer small, intimate settings. How would you design my home? Can you give me a rough sketch?"

Sandra's heart pounded. She would walk across West Texas barefoot, with no water, if Ms. Angelo asked her to. Taking the pencil, she balanced the pad on her lap.

28

"Sit over here," Ms. Angelo instructed, motioning to Ms. Dysan's desk.

Sandra tried not to notice the heat from Ms. Angelo's body as she eased by her. Sandra sat down and closed her eyes. She thought about what Ms. Angelo wanted. Slowly, the rooms formed in her mind's eye and began to come together. She opened her eyes, still seeing the scene going on inside her head. The pencil began to move, roughly sketching the home Ms. Angelo wanted.

She drew a spacious living room with a stone fireplace at one end. Tall, deep-set windows graced the living room walls.

In the master bedroom, a large window seat overlooked the back yard. Next to the window was a smaller, more intimate fireplace.

The kitchen was a simple design with French doors leading out to a trellised patio. Lost in the joy of her creation, Sandra rapidly penciled in crude outlines of furniture.

She closed the yard off with a short picket fence and added a doggie door to the back door. She drew a quick line sketch of two cats sitting on the window seat in the bedroom before blinking and gazing at the design before her.

She felt disappointed. The house was not majestic enough for Ms. Angelo. Unable to look up to see her disappointment, Sandra pushed the paper toward her. A hand reached out to take the pad.

"My God," Ms. Dysan breathed. "If I hadn't been standing here, I would not have believed it."

Sandra looked up to find the two women staring at each other and smiling. She looked away quickly and swallowed her pain at their closeness.

Finally, Ms. Dysan cleared her throat and pulled a side chair up close. "Sandra," she began, "have you given any thought to college?"

Embarrassed, Sandra stared down at her hands. There was no money to send her to college.

"I'm not going."

"Why not?" Ms. Angelo exclaimed. "Sandra, you have a very unusual talent. You could . . ."

From the corner of her eye, Sandra saw Ms. Dysan reach out and touch Ms. Angelo's hand and she fell silent.

Ms. Dysan placed the pad back on the desk before Sandra. "I think your grades alone are good enough to guarantee you at least a partial scholarship, but what I'd like to do is enter your model in an architectural design contest. Of course, I would need your father's permission to do so."

Not able to follow the turn of the conversation, Sandra frowned.

"Nancy, explain it to her," Ms. Angelo prodded.

"Every year the National Association for Women Architects sponsors a contest," Ms Dysan began. "It's opened to women between the ages of seventeen and twenty-five. They are looking for young women who show promising architectural skills. First prize is a full scholarship to your choice of three very prestigious colleges." She took a deep breath and smiled at Sandra. "We think you have a good chance of winning."

Sandra felt a mixture of excitement and fear. She refused to allow herself to want this. Caring would cause her pain when she lost.

"The deadline is January fifteenth," Ms. Angelo continued, "but your model is completed and I know we can get the paperwork ready in plenty of time."

"It's really up to you and your father," Ms. Dysan added.

"I'm sure he will be pleased. How do you feel about entering the contest?" Ms. Angelo queried, placing a hand on Sandra's shoulder. The jolt of pleasure shooting through her prevented Sandra from managing more than a nod. She had a vague feeling her father might not be as thrilled about the idea as Ms. Angelo was.

As it turned out, Sandra's father was more opposed to the idea than Sandra could have imagined. They had their one and only serious argument. Sandra held her ground and after two days of battle, he gave in.

Eight months later, Sandra hugged her father goodbye and climbed onto a bus with a full scholarship and the start to a career she never dreamed possible.

Laura's hand on Sandra's shoulder ended her reverie. "Are you okay?"

"Yeah." Sandra rubbed her face and glanced at her Rolex. "I'd better get home. Can you loan me cab fare?"

"I'll drive you," Laura said, reaching for her coat.

"No. Please. You hate driving in the city and you've already made the trip once."

Sandra stepped out of the cab wearing Laura's jogging suit and fuzzy, blue slippers. She approached her building acting as though there was nothing odd about her wardrobe.

"Good morning, Richard," Sandra said, holding her head high and shuffling passed the curious doorman. She took the elevator up and stood outside her penthouse door wishing she could slip in unnoticed, but her house key was on her key ring. She had no choice but to ring the bell. Taking a deep breath, she reached for the doorbell, knowing Carol would open the door since Margaret, the live-in maid, was off today.

Margaret and Carol were constantly at odds, but both understood the other was there to stay, so they worked around their differences in an uneasy truce. *Margaret is probably enjoying herself with her Canasta friends*, Sandra thought, and experienced a pang of mild jealousy at Margaret's freedom.

What would it be like to have a group of friends? She rang the doorbell again and waited as Carol took her sweet time in opening the door.

"Where have you been?" Carol demanded as she pulled the door open. Her face contorted in an ugly mask. "You made a complete fool of yourself last night. The phone's been ringing all morning with those snide bitches trying to get the latest news."

Sandra pushed past her, intending to escape to her office, but Carol trailed across the room after her. Not wanting Carol to follow her, Sandra stopped in the hallway. Sandra's home office was her sanctuary, the one place she could retreat to and relax.

Releasing a ragged breath, she turned to face Carol. "I'm sorry about last night, and I don't want to argue. Can we please not do this?"

"Who is she?" Carol demanded.

Sandra groaned. "There's no one else. How many times do I have to tell you?"

"Then where were you all night? I waited until practically everyone left, thinking you would come back for me. You made me look like a fool."

"I went for a walk. Just thinking." She would never tell Carol she spent the night sleeping in the park like a common vagrant. She doubted she would ever admit to calling Laura, since Carol would blow everything out of proportion.

Laura and Carol disliked each other from the very beginning. After a couple of disastrous dinners, Sandra decided to keep them in separate areas of her life. She stopped inviting Carol along when she went to visit Laura and only invited Laura over when Carol was out of town.

"And where did you get those horrid clothes?"

Sandra looked down at the too short pants. How was she going to explain this without mentioning Laura? Carol would never believe there was nothing more than friendship between them.

Sighing, she gave up. Carol deserved to know what had happened. It was time to sit down and talk about what was going on between them. She started to motion to the sofa when a tall, vaguely familiar blonde strolled from the hallway. Sandra caught the look of irritation on Carol's face.

"Beautiful bathroom," the blonde purred, arching her eyebrows at Carol before turning to Sandra. After slowly taking in Sandra's disheveled appearance, she smirked. "You must be Sandra. I'm Ingrid Bennington."

She was the woman Carol had been laughing with at Lona's party. Sandra turned to Carol for some hint as to why Ingrid was at the penthouse so early, but was shocked into silence by the look of cold fury on Carol's face. *I'm embarrassing her*, Sandra realized.

"Excuse me," Sandra said, and rushed down the hallway to her office. She tried to concentrate on a speech she was giving at a local high school later in the month, but she found herself returning to the window to stare aimlessly across the city. There had to be something more to life out there.

CHAPTER THREE

Makeup failed to camouflage the cut above Sandra's eye. As she drove to her office, she worked on a plausible lie to explain how she had received it.

At eight sharp, Allison Kramer, Sandra's senior project manager, walked in. A look of surprise crossed Allison's face when she noticed the cut over Sandra's eye, but in typical Allison-style she took a seat and began to review current projects. Sandra listened with only half her attention. The other half was busy trying to analyze her growing discontent.

"Sandra?"

She looked up to find Allison standing by her desk.

"Are you all right?"

"Uh. Yes. I'm sorry, Allison. I'm afraid I was thinking

about something else." She reached into her desk for the antacids she kept. All this worrying gave her heartburn.

"Is it something I can help with?" Allison brushed back a loose lock of her unruly red hair.

"No, but thanks." Sandra felt restless, unable to concentrate. "I just need some time. In fact, unless you have something urgent, let's wait until after lunch to go over these deadlines."

Allison began to gather her folders. "There's nothing really pressing," she said. She walked to the door and hesitated. "Sandra, if you need someone to talk to, I hope you know you can turn to me. I'll never forget what you did for me and my family."

Uncomfortable with the personal turn of the conversation, Sandra stood and tried to smile. "Thanks. I appreciate the offer, but really it's nothing."

Sandra saw the confusion on Allison's face as she turned to leave. Realizing she might have hurt her feelings Sandra quickly added, "Allison, you've more than earned everything you have. You're a hell of a worker. I've never regretted hiring you."

Allison's face brightened. "Thanks." She slipped out and left Sandra, already lost in memories, staring at the closed door.

Upon graduation, Sandra had received an internship with a major New York architectural firm. She worked hard and saved her money. Four years later, she returned to Dallas to start her own firm and be closer to her father.

As Sandra's fledgling firm began to grow, she ran an ad for a personal assistant. Allison Kramer, a big-boned woman with flaming red hair, arrived with her résumé listing little other than a business degree. Sandra interviewed other applicants with more impressive work records, but she felt an immediate liking for Allison's straightforward approach. She hired her after the initial interview. She would later learn that Allison's son, Brian, had been diagnosed with multiple sclerosis at the age of two. A week after hearing the diagnosis, Allison's husband went to buy a gallon of milk and kept driving. She faced the emotional and financial responsibility of raising Brian alone. Allison's mother tried to help, but she was barely surviving on the small pension check her husband left her.

As Tate Enterprises grew, so did Allison's responsibilities and compensation. After five years, she was able to hire a private nurse to stay with Brian and purchase a home large enough for her mother to live with them.

Sandra now depended on Allison for a multitude of things. As such, Allison knew almost as much about the affairs and operations of the company as Sandra.

The telephone rang, jarring Sandra from her reverie. She let her secretary, Betty, answer it and turned her attention to reviewing project deadlines. Her concentration drifted and her thoughts quickly turned to Carol.

A typical day for Carol revolved around beauty appointments, charity events, and luncheons.

Carol's father, Richard Grant, was the sole heir of the considerable Grant family dynasty. Unfortunately, he did not inherit the family's knack of maintaining the wealth. Through a long series of bad investments and living well beyond his means, he slowly lost the inheritance that should have proided Carol with lifelong luxury.

Shortly after she and Carol became lovers, Sandra discovered the Grants were struggling to maintain the façade of an endless source of money.

Sandra loaned Richard Grant money several times at Carol's urging. He made no offer of repaying the loans. Sandra's generosity stopped when realized she would soon be broke if she continued to support Richard Grant's lavish lifestyle.

Carol became enraged when she discovered Sandra would no longer loan him money. She secretly gave her father money from the account Sandra established for her. It never occurred to her that Sandra reviewed the statements.

Sandra had established the generously funded account to allow Carol a sense of independence, and since the financial gifts remained within the allotted amount, Sandra said nothing.

During their first year together, Sandra sensed an underlying sadness in Carol. She tried to encourage Carol to find something she liked to do, even if it was volunteer work. She hinted that Carol might enjoy the sense of fulfillment work provided.

Carol's response was anger and tears. She accused Sandra of trying to make her feel guilty about not working. Sandra gave up and left her alone.

A sharp pang of guilt stabbed Sandra. She did ignore Carol. Project deadlines and last minute meetings kept her working late most days. In fact, she and Carol rarely did anything together. She thought about the disaster at Lona's party and cringed. Appearances, both physical and social, meant so much to Carol.

The intercom interrupted her thoughts. "Yes, Betty."

"Mr. Carlton would like to see you. He says it's important."

Sandra groaned. Charles Carlton was a royal pain. She considered sending him away, but he was working on a major advertising campaign and the deadline was coming up. "Send him in." *What's he going to bitch about today?* she wondered.

Charles swept into her office in a cloud of expensive cologne and moved about as if the office was his own. He placed a stack of display boards on the sofa located on the far side of Sandra's office. The sofa was the anchoring point of an informal sitting area where Sandra often held briefings. Today his obtrusiveness irritated her more than usual. She sat at her desk pretending to study the report in front of her.

He sat on the sofa for a moment. When it became obvious

Sandra was not moving across the room to join him, he gathered up the display boards and placed them on a chair in front of her desk. Without waiting for an invitation, he settled himself in an adjoining chair. "Good morning," he boomed.

She delayed a heartbeat longer than was courteous before responding.

"Good morning, Charles. What did you need to see me about?" she began, trying to cut off any chance of chitchat.

His eyebrows shot up as he let out a short whistle. "Where'd you get that?" he asked, pointing to the wound above her eye.

Her hand moved to touch the cut before she could stop herself. "It's nothing. Did you have something you needed to see me about?"

He was on the verge of making another comment when she pierced him with the famous Tate glare. A flash of resentment crossed his face, but he hid it as he leaned over and retrieved the first of his boards.

"Here are the layouts for the Madison Medical Complex. I know we were going to review them at tomorrow's staff meeting, but I wanted to get your feedback." He held up a board displaying an extremely young woman who wore little more than a tool belt and held a screwdriver with its handle resting suggestively against her chin.

Sandra felt the burning in her stomach expand. She started to reach for another antacid, but stopped. She was taking too many. Suppressing her impatience, she asked, "Charles, what does this display have to do with doctors or dentists? Why have you brought these to me? You report to Gordon. You know everything should go through him first."

The Madison Medical Complex was a cluster of historic buildings Sandra discovered on one of her routine scouting drives. Whenever she had time or needed to get away from the office, she took random drives around the city looking for sites or buildings that appealed to her. Occasionally, she would discover a hidden jewel like what was to become the medical complex. The buildings were located near one of the larger hospitals and after renovation, Sandra planned to market them as office space for doctors and dentists.

Sandra studied Charles, wondering if he would ever change. Tate Enterprise hired him last year fresh out of college. He often irritated co-workers and showed weak customer skills, but he held promises of being Dallas' next advertising genius.

Unfortunately, Sandra had soon discovered most of Charles' advertising ideas revolved around subtle and sometimes not so subtle sex.

"Sandra, sex sells." He flashed her a smile meant to charm her, but it only served to irritate her more.

"Not at Tate Enterprises it doesn't. I've told you this is not the image I want portrayed. What else do you have?" He held up three more boards, all as bad as the first. Again she pushed her annoyance down, and caused her stomach a new wave of pain.

"Have you even shown these to Gordon?"

Gordon Wayne was the vice president of marketing. Charles should have taken the boards to him for approval.

"Yes, but you know how old fashioned Gordon is. I wanted to show you the designs. I knew you could better appreciate the need to sell."

"They won't do!" Sandra snapped, harsher than she intended.

Anger flushed his cheeks. He started to protest, but she held up her hand to stop his comment.

"Have something more appropriate prepared for the staff meeting tomorrow. You know what I'm looking for." She rose to signal the meeting was over.

He snatched up the boards. "I won't have time to work up new layouts by tomorrow."

Sandra leaned across her desk, her voice dropping drastically. "You knew what I wanted, and you've had two months to produce something. I want a new series of appropriate layouts by tomorrow. They are due to the printers on Monday morning. And Charles, if you want to continue with Tate Enterprises, I suggest you start listening."

He stormed out of her office without replying. As the door slammed behind him, the pains hit her, sharper and more intense. She fell back into her chair and clutched her chest. She struggled to breathe, fighting the fear gripping her. Slowly the pain subsided. She was chewing the last of the antacids when Allison came in.

"Sandra, I have the proposals . . ." She stopped in mid-sentence and ran to Sandra's desk. "What's wrong?"

Sandra shook her head, reaching for a tissue to wipe the sweat from her face.

"Should I call a doctor?" Allison reached for the telephone.

"No. It's just something I ate. I'll be fine."

Allison looked at her doubtfully.

"I'm fine," Sandra insisted, her voice growing firmer. "It's only heartburn. Charles just left," she added, as if that should explain everything.

"You don't look *fine*," Allison replied. "I think you should see a doctor. You've lost weight and you eat antacids like they were candy. You look tired, Sandra."

"It's nothing." She tried to straighten the papers on her desk, but her hands shook noticeably.

Allison reached over and removed the papers from Sandra's hands. "I can't afford a dead boss. Either you agree to go to the doctor, or I drive you home where you can rest. Which will it be?"

Sandra was too tired to argue. The latest attack scared her.

"Home," she relented, "but I can drive myself. I need you to sit in for me at the ten o'clock briefing with Dunbar. He wants to discuss some structural changes required before we can receive city approval. Andrea is the designer and she will be there. I was only going to make an appearance of goodwill to show the firm is willing to incorporate any changes they deem necessary."

"Let me get someone to drive you."

Sandra stood. "I can drive myself," she stated. Her tone was sharper than she intended. To soften the words she patted Allison's arm and said, "I won't die on you." She took her purse from her desk. "At least not until we've met all our deadlines." She gave a weak smile and left.

Sandra drove straight home, and was surprised to see Carol's car in the garage. She assumed Carol would be gone to whatever she did during the day.

Mondays were Margaret's shopping day, so she would be out most of the day.

Sandra let herself in with her key and removed her jacket. She thought about working in her study for awhile, but was suddenly too exhausted. She had not slept well the previous two nights.

All I need is a few hours of sleep, she reasoned as she headed down the hallway to the bedroom she and Carol shared. They had not spoken since their brief encounter yesterday. Carol had disappeared after Sandra escaped to her office and not returned home until after midnight. They spent a long silent night clinging to their respective sides of the bed. Carol was still sleeping when Sandra left for work.

If she's in, perhaps we can talk, Sandra thought. *We have to clear this up. After I've rested for an hour or so, we can go somewhere for the afternoon and maybe even share an early dinner.* Sandra opened the bedroom door gently, in case Carol was still sleeping. She stopped short at the spectacle before her. Carol sat in the middle of their bed, with her head thrown back, moaning in ecstasy. A blond tangle of hair spread out from between her legs and across the bed. A cry began and died in the back of Sandra's throat.

Carol's eyes flew open. A look of sheer terror crossed her face. Sandra felt her feet weld themselves to the floor. She could only stare at the woman between Carol's legs. All the times she tried to get Carol to let her touch her came back in a flash. How long had she been seeing this woman? Was she the first or were there others? Was this how Carol normally spent her days?

"Sandra, I can explain," Carol said, crawling across the bed toward her. Ingrid Bennington sat up and tossed her mane of wild hair, her lips still wet with Carol's excitement. She flashed Sandra a triumphant smile.

Carol grabbed Sandra's hand. "It's not what it looks like."

Sandra looked down into Carol's face. She had been such a fool! "You have exactly five minutes to get out. Get dressed. Don't bother packing."

"Sandra! No!" Carol began to cry. "Please, let me explain. Ingrid is a photographer. She came by to take my photo and . . . and . . ."

"Four minutes," Sandra said, feeling made of stone.

"You can't do this! You can't make me leave. This is my home, too."

"You signed away your title when you let that bitch crawl between your legs," Sandra spat. "You're down to three minutes. Unless you want to walk through the lobby as you are now, I suggest you start dressing."

Ingrid slid from the bed and began to dress with slow deliberation. Sandra tore away from Carol and crossed the room to where Carol's purse sat on the dresser. She began to dig through it.

"What are you doing?" Carol demanded.

"I'm taking my car keys and my credit cards."

"What am I supposed to do?" Carol wailed.

"You can either crawl back to Daddy, live with the love of your life there," she said, pointing to Ingrid. "Or you can get a job." She glared at Carol, who stood naked before her. The initial shock was wearing off, and Carol's anger was building.

"You can't do this to me," she insisted. Her voice shook as she continued. "I'll sue you for everything you have."

"No, you won't. You'd have to admit you're a lesbian. What would Daddy do then?"

Carol's arm swung up to slap her. Sandra caught it and pushed it aside. Carol grabbed a suit from her closet and began to dress. As soon as she pulled the skirt and blouse on, Sandra threw the purse to her.

"Get out of my house and take your trash with you," she said, tilting her head to indicate Ingrid.

"You'll be sorry," Carol hissed.

"I've been sorry for years," Sandra countered. She waited until she heard the front door slam before she reached for the telephone and called the building security guard.

"Hello, Richard. This is Sandra Tate. Ms. Grant no longer resides here. She should be leaving the building in a few seconds. She's not to be allowed back in under any circumstances."

It took Sandra three telephone calls to get Ingrid Bennington's address. An hour later, a moving crew arrived at Sandra's penthouse and packed Carol's things. Sandra gave them Ingrid's address and signed a check, which included a hefty bonus for their willingness to arrive on such short notice. A separate courier arrived to transport Carol's jewelry.

Sandra systematically canceled Carol's credit cards, charge accounts, and bank accounts. After the last call, she forwarded her calls to the answering service and allowed herself a rare shot of Scotch. She carried it to one of the guest bedrooms where she stripped and crawled into bed. She pushed all thoughts of Carol from her mind, downed the Scotch, and was soon asleep.

CHAPTER FOUR

Sandra opened her eyes to an unfamiliar room. Disoriented and bewildered, she looked around the darkened room and moaned as the events of the past few hours slammed back. Her throat constricted as the look of ecstasy on Carol's face came back to haunt her.

Why was I never able to put it there? she wondered. *Carol was right. I am a lousy lover.*

For years, she had held onto her belief that Carol's lack of interest in sex caused their problems. Now, she knew it was not Carol.

She was the problem.

Sandra tried to analyze her feelings for Carol, but they were too complicated and clouded. Had she ever loved Carol?

Yes, in the beginning, before she discovered Carol tricked her and used her as a money tool to help her father.

Sandra glanced at the glowing digits on the clock beside the bed. It was already after ten; she slept the entire day away. She pulled the blanket from the bed, wrapped it around her, and walked aimlessly around the room. Unable to corral her thoughts, she opened the French doors and stepped out onto the dark balcony. The late February temperatures were brisk, but Sandra craved its freshness.

She curled into a chair and deliberately avoided thinking about Carol. At some point she would have to come to terms with her, but the wound was still too raw. She focused her thoughts on work until the cold drove her back inside.

Chilled, she slipped on a bathrobe and headed to the kitchen to make herself a cup of coffee.

"Ah, there you are, lass. Will you be wantin' to eat now?"

Startled by the voice, Sandra jumped. "Margaret. What are you doing awake? It's almost midnight."

Margaret started working for Sandra about a month after Sandra and Carol got together. Carol insisted they hire a maid. Sandra had been hesitant to let a stranger into her home, until one of Carol's friends mentioned they were moving back to London and their housekeeper refused to go with them. The woman assured Sandra that Margaret was discreet. Sandra soon discovered the reason Margaret so calmly accepted her employer's lesbian lifestyle: Margaret was a lesbian herself.

An immediate bond developed with the stout, no-nonsense woman who even after several years of living in the States still spoke with a strong Irish brogue. The bond flourished, and a deep sense of respect and caring developed between the two women.

"I thought you and your Canasta buddy, Minnie, were going to a wedding tonight."

"So we were, lass, but Minnie was feeling poorly and we decided not to go." She pulled bowls from the refrigerator.

"Margaret, I'm not hungry. I came out to get a cup of coffee."

Margaret looked at her critically. "You've not had your supper, I'll wager."

"I'm really not hungry."

Margaret was about to protest, but Sandra shot her a warning glance. Never one to be intimidated, Margaret anchored her hands on her hips. "Ms. Grant won't be liking your drinking coffee at this hour."

Sandra suppressed a groan. Somehow, Margaret must have already heard the rumors and canceled her plans with Minnie to make sure Sandra was all right. She was now waiting for Sandra to confirm the rumors.

Sandra plopped onto a stool and rubbed her hands over her face. It would be days before Margaret stopped saying "I told you so". "Ms. Grant doesn't live here any more and quite frankly never gave a damn what I ate or drank when she was here." Sandra watched in surprise as a kaleidoscope of emotions danced over Margaret's face. She knew Margaret disliked Carol as much as Carol disapproved of Margaret.

Carol accused Sandra of treating Margaret like family. Sandra had laughed and told her she wished Margaret were family. The statement caused an unpleasant scene, and Carol only resented Margaret more.

"Are you okay, lass?" Margaret asked with such concern a lump formed in Sandra's throat. She swallowed several times, fighting to regain control of her emotions.

"I'm fine," she said. "It should have ended years ago. We've both been dragging it out too long."

The intercom buzzer from the security guard interrupted them.

"Now, who would come calling at this hour?" Margaret scolded as she went to answer. Sandra followed.

"Ms. Cromwell is here to see Ms. Tate. She says it's urgent," Arnold, the night security guard, informed them in what Sandra secretly called his Humphrey Bogart voice. In his early sixties, Arnold was always ready to tell anyone, who made the mistake of lingering within hearing distance, about his golden years in Hollywood.

Margaret waited for Sandra to decide whether to allow Lona to come up or not.

Sandra considered brushing Lona off, but if Lona said it was urgent, it probably was.

"Send her up," she said, earning another glare of disapproval from Margaret.

"You should be in bed. Not havin' to listen to the likes of that bloody woman."

"Margaret, I'll be fine. Go on to bed and make sure you give Minnie my best tomorrow when you talk to her."

Margaret was gearing up for a battle, but Sandra cut her off. "You let me know if she starts feeling worse," Sandra said. "I'll stop by to see her on my way home tomorrow and take her some flowers to cheer her up." The ploy stopped the softhearted Margaret cold, as Sandra knew it would.

"Ah, bless you. You're so busy, but still take time to care for others. You're too good for this old world," Margaret said with a sniff. She dabbed her eyes as she made her way to her room.

Sandra shook her head and made a mental note to check on Minnie's progress. The doorbell rang and she went to answer it.

"Sandra, darling. Are you all right?" Lona Cromwell floated through the doorway and pulled Sandra into a crushing embrace.

"I'm fine," Sandra said, maneuvering herself away from Lona's arms.

"I was so shocked when I heard the news."

Sandra's face burned. The news spread much more quickly than she anticipated. How? Considering Carol's distaste for gossip, she doubted it came from her. That left Ingrid Bennington.

"You poor thing," Lona cooed, and reached for her again.

Sandra avoided the hug by executing a quick turn toward the kitchen.

"I was about to make some coffee. Would you like a cup?"

"No, dear. You know I detest coffee. Tell Margaret I'll have tea."

"Margaret's already in bed, but I'll fix you a cup."

Lona shook her head and clamped onto Sandra's arm. "You need someone to take care of you. You're entirely too lax on your household. You need to rule with a firm hand."

"Lona, I'm perfectly capable of fixing myself a cup of coffee."

"I wasn't just referring to your household staff," she replied, giving Sandra a knowing glance.

Clueless, Sandra stopped and stared at her. "What are you talking about?"

"You're such an innocent." Her hand pushed the hair back from Sandra's face. "You may be a financial genius, but you know nothing about what women want."

Sandra felt her face turn scarlet. *Has Carol told the whole world I'm lousy lover?*

"Look at you," Lona chuckled, increasing Sandra's discomfort.

"I don't have your experience, I'm sure," Sandra snapped, yanking her arm away as she made her escape to the kitchen.

Lona Cromwell's reputation spread much farther than Texas. Long ago, Sandra stopped trying to keep up with all the rumors.

Lona followed her, seemingly unaffected by her remarks. Sandra smiled when she found a sandwich sitting on the counter alongside a pot of coffee. Margaret had again gotten the last word.

"Did it ever occur to you, I move from woman to woman because I couldn't have what I truly wanted?" Lona asked as she continued to approach Sandra.

"And what might that be?" Sandra asked. She tried to ignore Lona's closeness as she searched the pantry for tea.

"You." A hand trailed slowly down her back and Sandra shivered in spite of herself. She turned and backed up trying to get away, but Lona trapped her against the pantry. "I've waited for you to notice me for so long, but you could never see beyond Carol."

"Lona, stop it." Sandra tried to move past her, but Lona held her space and continued.

"I knew you weren't happy. I could see the sadness in your eyes. And her screwing every woman who showed the slightest interest."

Sandra flinched. There it was. Ingrid was not Carol's first affair. She wanted to know who the other women were, but could not bring herself to ask. Lona was still talking.

"She never knew how to treat you, but I do." Her hands were on Sandra's waist. "I can make you feel like the powerful woman you are. I would do anything you told me. Anything."

Where is this going? Sandra wondered.

"Tell me what you want," Lona whispered in a sultry voice. Her lips brushed against Sandra's ear. "You deserve it. Whatever it might be. I'm yours for the taking."

In spite of her revulsion, Sandra felt a part of herself responding. Her robe opened and Lona's hands roamed over her bare skin. Lona's lips inched down Sandra's throat and trailed a burning line between her breasts before she stopped to whisper in Sandra's ear. "Take control. Make me please you."

Sandra felt a stab of excitement course through her. *Don't do this*, she warned herself as she grabbed Lona's hands and tried to push her away. The last thing she needed now was to become involved with Lona Cromwell. Sandra wished her body was as reasonable as her brain.

"Yes," Lona moaned when Sandra's grip tightened.

"Lona, stop it." Sandra shook her. "I want you to go home."

"No," Lona cried, her face distorted in anguish. "I want you to control me. I need you. I'm bad. You need to punish me!"

Sandra watched mesmerized as Lona unzipped her jumper and slid it off her shoulders to reveal herself to Sandra. Each pierced nipple held a small gold ring connected by a thin golden chain.

"For you," Lona cooed.

Sandra closed her eyes and tried to control the desire sweeping through her. *I'm doing this because of Carol,* she told herself. *She made me feel powerless and I'm only reacting to Lona because I need the control back in my life.*

No matter how much she talked to herself, her desire for Lona escalated. She shoved Lona away, ill and ashamed of the lust pounding her body. Lona slipped to the floor.

Sandra collapsed onto a stool and dropped her head to the cool wood of the counter. She had almost given in. Lona's submission had excited her, but the sight of her pierced and chained body also shocked Sandra.

Lona groaned. For one heart-stopping second Sandra thought she might be physically hurt. She started to rise, but Lona stopped her with a smoldering glance.

"I knew you would respond," Lona said hoarsely, and crawled to Sandra. Lona's face held a look that both attracted and frightened Sandra.

"Let me thank you," Lona begged.

Sandra sat transfixed as Lona crawled to her. In one swift move, Lona spread Sandra's legs and buried her head between Sandra's thighs. She wanted to protest, but Lona's tongue was creating magic previously unknown to Sandra. She gave in to the hunger consuming her. Desperate for the release offered by Lona, Sandra wrapped her hands in Lona's long black hair and pulled her tighter against her throbbing center. Lona moaned and moved as if possessed. Sandra slipped to the edge of the stool and rode Lona's tongue until she dropped over the edge of sensation and swirled unimpeded through a warm void.

She sat stunned with her hands wrapped in Lona's hair, while Lona contentedly licked away Sandra's juices.

Sandra was scared. For the second time in less than twenty-four hours, she had lost control. She glanced down at the tangle of Lona's hair between her legs. How would she ever be able to face this woman again? *We both wanted it*, she reminded herself. Nevertheless, this was definitely not something she intended to continue. Lona's busy tongue made it difficult for her to concentrate on anything.

Lona was the kind of woman who would be attracted to anything she saw as unattainable. With her goal achieved, perhaps she would lose interest. There was still the matter of getting her out of the house and quickly, Sandra thought. *Control. She wants to be controlled.* Lona started to look up.

"Don't look at me." Sandra forced as much brusqueness into her voice as possible. Lona immediately dropped her head and lowered her body. Sandra gritted her teeth. *Be persuasive.* "I'm through with you," Sandra snapped. "Go home and don't bother me again." She half expected Lona to rise and slap her; instead, Lona crawled out of the kitchen. A few seconds later, Sandra heard the front door open and close.

Sandra felt ill and ran down the hall to the bathroom. She had not eaten anything since breakfast and suffered a spasm of dry heaves. Having witnessed a side of herself she never knew existed scared her.

Sandra washed her face and rinsed her mouth. As she dried her face, she was shocked to find dark circles ringing her eyes. The cut above her eye glowed red and angry-looking against her pale skin. She released a long sigh, admitting she felt as tired as she looked.

The tightness in her chest began again. She slowly made her way back to the guest room and lay on the bed with extra pillows piled behind her head to alleviate the pressure building in her chest.

She stared at the ceiling until the pressure subsided. The eastern sky grew light before she slipped into a restless sleep.

She slept less than an hour. Thoughts of Lona and Carol banged around inside her skull. It would be useless to try and go back to sleep. She took a hot shower and spent extra time on her makeup to hide the circles beneath her eyes.

She entered the kitchen to find Margaret in a tiff. *I didn't eat the sandwich*, she groaned with a mixture of guilt and shame at the reason she had forgotten it. She decided to bluff her way through. "Good morning," she called in a voice much cheerier than she felt. "Margaret, you were absolutely right."

Margaret eyed her suspiciously. When Sandra failed to elaborate, her curiosity got the best of her. "And how might that be, lass?"

"You said all I needed was a good night's sleep. After Lona left, I went to bed and slept like a baby."

"Then you'll be a wantin' breakfast?" Once again, Margaret had out maneuvered her.

"That sounds good," Sandra agreed, trying to ignore the queasy toss of her stomach.

Margaret placed toast and a bowl of fruit before her. Sandra pasted a look of contentment on her face and pretended to study the newspaper while she forced herself to eat.

She chewed several antacids on her way to work. The food sat heavily in her stomach. It was time to call Dr. Rayburn. The heartburn would not go away, and the pains in her chest were occurring more frequently. *I'll call after this morning's staff meeting*, she promised herself. Dr. Ida Rayburn would make time for her.

Sandra heard Betty's excited voice seconds before her office door flew open. Carol stormed in with Lynda Hopkins, a divorce lawyer who specialized in palimony cases.

"I'm sorry," Betty said. "I tried to stop them."

Sandra waved her off. "It's okay, Betty. Hold my calls."

Betty nodded and cast a suspicious glance at the two intruders.

"So this is where the great Sandra Tate holds court," Carol said gazing around Sandra's almost utilitarian office.

Sandra realized Carol had never before visited her office. She wondered how many of her employees even knew she lived with a woman.

"It's even worse than I ever imagined, but I'm not surprised." Carol cut into her speculation. "People like you never have any taste."

Sandra glanced around her office. One side was taken up with a large drafting table and work center. Her walnut desk with its brown tweed side chairs sat in front of a large window from which she could see downtown Dallas. The sofa, two armchairs, and a long coffee table that served as her informal conference area completed the furniture of the room. A wide array of artwork from generally unknown artists decorated the pale beige walls.

She shrugged off Carol's remarks and offered them a chair.

Lynda seemed somewhat embarrassed. "I'm sorry to have to do this here," she told Sandra. "I usually prefer to meet in my office, but Carol has hired me to represent her."

"Let's get on with this," Carol hissed. She studied her nails to avoid eye contact with Sandra.

Lynda sat her briefcase on her lap and removed a sheaf of papers. "Sandra, we've drawn up a financial . . ."

"Let me save you some time," Sandra interrupted. "She's not getting anything more than she's already received."

"See? I told you," Carol shouted triumphantly at Lynda, who seemed shocked by Sandra's response.

"Nothing." Sandra turned to Carol. The tightness in her chest increased. She forced herself to take deep breaths before she continued. "For eight long years, I listened to you accuse me of being unfaithful, when apparently you were judging me by your own actions. I tried to encourage you to find something you liked to do and if Monday was any example, you obviously did. You chose Ingrid Bennington, so go live with her. I'm not giving you another penny."

"Ms. Tate," Lynda prompted, assuming her lawyer's stance. "My client will be forced to take you to court."

Sandra sighed. She had known Lynda Hopkins for ten years, and now they were opposing each other because of Carol's greed. There was no way to explain to Lynda that giving in to Carol would result in a lifelong commitment of conceding to her demands. It would not stop with the first settlement. Carol would never be satisfied. She would always want more.

"Lynda, she's free to do as she wishes, but I won't willingly give her anything."

"Sandra." Lynda dropped the façade. "Having your relationship made public would hurt both of you. Why not listen to our proposal? It's simply a matter of a yearly income. Once you hear our offer, I think you will agree it's fair. Don't you think Carol deserves something for the eight years she stood by you?"

"Stood by me! You make her sound like some fifties housewife." She glared at Carol. "Why don't you tell me exactly what you did for me, earning you the right to be supported for the rest of your life?"

"I stayed home alone and waited for you to find time for me," Carol accused, as fake tears filled her eyes.

"You may have been home, but you certainly weren't alone."

"I got lonesome and made one mistake. If you came home as you should this never would have happened," Carol sniffed.

"One mistake?" She held Carol's gaze. "Would you like for me to name a few more of your *mistakes,* or would you prefer to spare the women in question? Trust me, Carol. If this goes to court, I won't spare anyone." She silently thanked Lona for the hint of Carol's other indiscretions. She waited as Carol tried to decide if Sandra's threats were bluffs. Sandra knew she was correct when Carol's face grew red with anger.

"At least someone wanted me," Carol hissed. "I knew all along you weren't having affairs and do you know why?"

Sandra braced herself. She knew Carol was going to hit her were she would hurt the worst, her own insecurities.

"No one wanted you," Carol taunted. "They never have and never will. Even your own mother didn't want you."

"Carol!" Lynda gasped.

Sandra reeled under the barrage as Carol continued. "The only thing you've ever been any good at is making money. You pathetic, low-bred bitch." Carol spun on her heels and stormed out the door.

Sandra and Lynda sat in stunned silence. Each of them stared at the door Carol slammed behind her.

"I'm sorry," Lynda finally mumbled. "She told me you were seeing other women and kicked her out with nothing."

"Careful, counselor. That sounds like privileged client information," Sandra whispered, willing the pain from her chest.

"Sandra, I'm really sorry. I never expected her to react this way. All those horrible things she said."

"They're all true," Sandra said softly and closed her eyes, as the clamp around her chest tightened.

"Sandra, are you all right?"

Sandra opened her eyes and nodded, unable to speak around the emotional pain clogging her throat. "I'm fine."

Lynda looked unconvinced.

"Really," Sandra assured her, offering a weak smile. They remained silent for a long second before Lynda began to stuff the papers back into her briefcase.

"There are a couple of things she says she didn't get," Lynda said as she closed her briefcase.

"What things?"

"Her birth certificate and passport."

Sandra nodded. "They are in the wall safe. I forgot them. I'll courier them over to you tomorrow morning." She forced herself to stand. "I'm sorry to rush you, but I'm late for a staff meeting."

Lynda nodded. "Tomorrow will be fine." She closed her briefcase and stood. "I want you to know, none of this is personal. I respect you and your commitment to the Dallas community."

Sandra shrugged. "Tell Carol if she insists on continuing with this, I'll see her in court."

"Sandra, I sincerely hope it won't come to that," Lynda said, as she turned and walked swiftly out the door.

Sandra shifted in her chair as one after the other of her board officers droned on about budgets and deadlines. Normally she would have been interested in the reports, but the pain in her chest was making it difficult for her to breathe. She groaned inwardly when Charles Carlton stood.

"I have four layouts to present. After we chose one I'll provide you the scheduled release dates," he informed everyone as he placed the first board on the easel.

Shocked, Sandra could only stare. Charles was presenting the same offensive layout of the young woman wearing the tool belt. The layout she ordered him to get rid of. She was on her feet, aware of the shocked surprise of everyone in the room.

"Charles, I specifically told you yesterday I did not want this trash used to represent any aspect of Tate Enterprises. Would you please explain to me why I'm seeing it again?"

"Sandra, I felt you weren't being objective. I wanted to let the board decide."

She glanced at each of the ten members seated around the table to see if any were in collusion with Charles. From their expressions, Sandra could tell they were as stunned as she was. She turned to Allison and saw disbelief in her eyes as well. Sandra's anger with Charles flamed brighter.

She stalked around the table and snatched the offensive board off the stand. She folded the board in half over her knee and dropped it into a trashcan. "I told you yesterday to have a layout I could use today."

To her surprise, he covered the distance to the trashcan in three strides and snatched the board out.

"This is good material and you won't even give it a chance," he shouted. His breath came in short hard puffs as he attempted to smooth the creases from the board.

"It's trash and I won't have it," Sandra shot back.

He poked her arm with his finger. "You're too fucking dense to know . . ."

Gordon Wayne leapt from his chair so swiftly it toppled over. "Charles!" he thundered. "In my office now!"

Charles reported to Gordon. Sandra knew she should let him handle it, but she could not get past the feeling of no longer being able to control even the smallest detail of her life. She raised her arm to stop Gordon. As she did so, her chest felt as though it ripped open. She fell backward from the impact of the pain. Her hands clawed at her chest as she gasped for breath. She tried to stand, but was unable to get her body to respond.

Allison's face hovered above her. She was talking to her, but Sandra was unable to hear. She tried to speak. No sound came out. She heard a voice screaming for someone to call 911. People stared down at her; their voices receded to a hollow hum as the room darkened. *I'm dying and I never got to live.*

A steady series of beeps was the first thing she heard. She opened her eyes to an array of monitors and Dr. Ida Rayburn's calm, brown eyes.

"You're no angel, so I must be in hell," Sandra joked weakly.

"Worse," Ida returned, making a notation on her chart. "You're still alive. That means you not only get my bill, but my lecture as well. Why haven't you been in to see me before today? And don't tell me the pains just started," she ordered, pointing a short, well-manicured finger at Sandra.

"I was going to call you after the meeting."

Ida peered at her closely. "The pain had already gotten that bad, huh?"

Sandra nodded.

"Tell me what's been going on with you," Ida said.

"There's been some pain. I've been plagued with heart-burn on and off for the last few days," Sandra said. "Is it my heart?" The implications of a heart attack were frightening.

Ida folded her arms. "No. You experienced a major anxiety attack."

Sandra almost cried with relief.

"Don't get excited too fast," Ida scolded. "I don't have the results from all the tests yet, but from what I've seen so far, you're damn lucky it wasn't your heart."

Sandra felt a moment of panic slice through her. The monitor began to beep loudly.

Ida placed a hand on Sandra's shoulder. "Relax. I don't mean to frighten you, but it's time you started thinking about your health. Take a deep breath."

Sandra did as she was told.

"And another one," Ida instructed.

Sandra continued to breathe deeply until the monitor resumed its steady blip.

"Now," Ida said. "Let me explain what I suspect is going on, and then we can spend the rest of the day arguing about what you're going to do about it." She stopped for a moment and tapped her pen against Sandra's chart. "This is a little unusual, but Allison Kramer is waiting outside and I'd like to call her in."

Sandra hesitated. She failed to see the need to discuss her medical condition with Allison, but Ida would never have asked without a good reason. Sandra felt a chill run over her body. "All right. If you think there's a need."

Ida stepped to the door, and a moment later Allison came in. Her eyes and nose were red from crying.

"How are you feeling?" she asked, placing her hand on Sandra's arm.

"Fine." Sandra's voice betrayed her fear.

"Allison, I wanted you in here while I talked to Sandra because I think I'll need your help to convince her of a few things." Ida flipped open Sandra's chart and thumbed through the pages.

"Sandra, your blood pressure is unbelievably high. I imagine part of the problem is due to all the excitement, so I'm going to have it monitored closely." She flipped to another page. "Your initial blood work shows me you're not eating properly. Your cholesterol is up, you're anemic, and you appear to be physically exhausted. This has been going on for more than a few days, hasn't it?" She fixed Sandra with an accusatory glare.

Sandra gave a guilty nod.

"What about the heartburn? She eats antacids like candy," Allison said.

Sandra felt betrayed by Allison's disclosures. She frowned to show her disapproval, but Allison ignored her.

Ida moved to the side of the bed and studied the machines monitoring Sandra. "How often was the pain occurring?"

"It's not bad."

Ida's stern glance stopped her. "Sandra, if you want to kill yourself, there are faster ways. Now, drop the martyr act and answer my questions."

Sandra blushed. Avoiding Ida's eyes, she hesitantly disclosed her symptoms.

Ida interrupted her several times to extract more details. When Sandra had told her everything, Ida turned to Allison.

"The reason I called you in was to enlist your help in getting Sandra to take a vacation."

Allison stepped closer to the bed. "I think it's a wonderful idea. We can handle things for a few days."

Sandra held up her hands. "Ida, after what happened today you don't need Allison's help. I'm more than willing to take a week or two off."

Ida looked at her gravely. "I'm not talking about a week or two. I'm thinking three or four months."

Sandra stared at her in disbelief. Even Allison hesitated.

"I can't leave for three months." Sandra tried to sit up. The beeping of the heart monitor began to race, and the tightness across her chest increased.

"Calm down or you'll have a nurse in here reading me the riot act," Ida admonished. She pushed Sandra gently back on the bed.

"Allison, tell her," Sandra directed.

Allison looked at Sandra and then at Ida. "Is it that serious?"

"I wouldn't have prescribed it otherwise. She's exhausted. If her blood pressure doesn't come down, she's a prime candidate for a stroke."

"Hello," Sandra piped in. "I'm right here, so don't talk about me as though I'm not."

Allison looked at her. "Dr. Rayburn's right. The board can run Tate Enterprises for a few months."

"Allison!"

"Damn it, Sandra. I'd rather we try to run it without you for a few months than have to bury you!" Allison shouted, and quickly looked away as the other two women stared at her in surprise. "You know I'd never find another job that pays as well as this one does," she teased with a small self-conscious smile.

Sandra lay stunned. How could she be away from work for three months? What would she do with herself?

She recalled lying on the boardroom floor thinking she was

dying. There could be other advantages to getting away for a while. She would be able to avoid both Carol and Lona. The news about her hospitalization would spread. It would appear she was resting rather than running away. Disappearing for a few months might be exactly what she needed.

"All right," she conceded so calmly both Ida and Allison eyed her doubtfully. "I'm serious," she assured them. "Allison, call a board meeting tomorrow morning and announce I'm going to take an extended vacation. You are in charge." Seeing Allison hesitate, she added. "You can handle things. You've worked with me long enough to know what I would or would not approve of." She turned to Ida and swallowed her guilt in taking the easy way out. "You happy now?" she asked.

"I think you must have hit your head when you fell," Ida said speculatively. "I expected more of a fight from you."

"No fight, Ida. You win."

CHAPTER FIVE

Ida insisted on keeping her overnight for observation. Sandra felt it prudent not to argue. They moved her to a private room, where she dozed to the monotonous beep of the heart monitor. The faint squeak of the door hinge roused her.

"Hello," Lona called, timidly stepping into the room.

The heart monitor's blip increased proportionally with Sandra's racing pulse as a wave of emotions washed over her. "Hi," she managed to stutter, unable to hold Lona's gaze.

Lona stopped just inside the room. An awkward silence fell between them. The spell was broken as the door swished open and a nurse rushed in.

"Is everything all right?" she threw Lona a quick glance, turning her full attention to the protesting monitor.

"I'm sorry," Sandra said. "I guess I sat up too quickly or something," she finished lamely.

The nurse checked the wires leading from the monitor to Sandra's arm.

"Take it a little easier next time," the nurse said, patting Sandra's arm before leaving the room.

Lona approached the bed and placed a single yellow rose on Sandra's lap. "I didn't know how you felt about flowers," she stated meekly. "I, ah . . . damn," she sputtered.

Sandra looked up to find tears in Lona's eyes. "What's wrong?"

"I wasn't sure you'd see me after last night."

Sandra started to speak, but Lona shook her head and stopped her. "I know what happened between us wasn't your scene, but I've dreamed about you for so long. When I heard Carol moved out, I told myself I was only going over to comfort you. Then you opened the door in your robe, and I couldn't stop myself." She pulled a tissue from her purse and wiped her eyes.

Sandra forced herself not to look away. "You gave me a lot to think about," she admitted. "I've never found myself in a situation like last night. Control has always been important to me." Seeing a gleam spark in Lona's eyes, she quickly added, "In my work I mean. I never, we never should have . . ." She trailed off into an uneasy silence.

"I realized I misjudged you after you sent me away," Lona responded.

Sandra felt a stab of mortification. She seemed to be a total failure at everything involving sex. She knew her face was glowing, and to add to her embarrassment, the damn machine was broadcasting her slightest agitation.

"It's all right," Lona said, taking Sandra's hand. "I want you to know, for a few minutes last night you gave me a glimpse of something I've been fantasizing about for years."

"What?" Sandra asked, stunned.

"When you wrapped my hair around your hands and rode

63

my mouth I was able to imagine what it would be like to be totally dominated by you. The memory of last night will provide me more fantasies than any real person ever could." She leaned forward and softly kissed Sandra's lips.

The blaring monitor again betrayed Sandra. "I guess there's something wrong with the machine," Sandra mumbled as they both glanced at it.

Lona gave her a wicked smile. "I'm sure there is." She hesitated before adding, "I hope we can still be friends."

Sandra could only nod.

Lona turned to leave but stopped at the door. "If you ever change your mind, call me." Without waiting for a reply, she winked and floated out of the room, just as the now exasperated-looking nurse returned.

A red-eyed and drawn-looking Margaret arrived soon after Lona's departure. She came bearing a thermos of homemade chicken soup.

"Dr. Rayburn told me I could bring this over," she said, pouring a small portion into a bowl. "I trimmed off the fat, like the doctor said. I knew they wouldn't be feedin' you proper," she continued. She hovered by the bed until Sandra finished most of the bowl.

Unable to contain herself any longer, Margaret shook her head. "You nearly scared the life out of me," she scolded and gathered up the soup bowl and thermos.

"I'm sorry," Sandra apologized, patting her hand.

"You'll not be scarin' me like that again now, will you?"

"No. I'm going to be so careful, when I get out of here, I'll live to be a hundred."

"Good. Good." Margaret blinked away tears. "For you gave me a fright for sure."

Sandra could only stare. Margaret was genuinely worried about her. With a start, she realized there were people who worried about her. They were concerned about Sandra Tate the person, not Sandra Tate the successful businesswoman. In a blinding flash of insight, she realized she had walked around in a vacuum her whole life, holding herself apart. With Laura being the only possible exception, she never allowed herself to trust anyone's friendship.

She even held a portion of herself from Laura. There was always a part of herself held in reserve.

"My heart," she whispered in surprise. "I've never allowed anyone into my heart."

"Your heart!" Poor Margaret was already racing to the door. "I'll find a nurse."

"No. Wait. Come back. I was talking to myself. I'm fine. Really."

Margaret eyed her. "For sure?"

Sandra smiled and said. "Yes. For sure."

Sandra felt something change inside of her — a subtle softening which made her smile bigger and made her want to make Margaret smile.

Sandra squeezed Margaret's hand. "How could I leave when I have a beautiful woman like you waiting for me at home?"

Margaret blushed a deep crimson, but smiled in spite of herself.

"You tell Minnie she'd better watch her step. I'm a single woman, and I might decide to steal you away from her."

Margaret hissed a flustered but pleased admonishment.

"Enough of your fancy talk. I've work to do. Will you be home tomorrow?"

"Only if you promise to be there to fluff my pillow," Sandra said with a lewd smile.

Margaret shook her finger at her and huffed. "Had the likes of Margaret O'Shea ever fluffed your pillows, lass, you would've been home much sooner each evenin'." With a defiant toss of her head, Margaret made a stately exit.

Seconds later, Ida Rayburn swept in with Sandra's chart. *So much for rest*, Sandra thought wearily.

"Was that Margaret I saw leaving?" Ida asked.

"Yes. She brought me a thermos of homemade chicken soup."

Ida nodded and chuckled. "She called me earlier and made it clear she didn't trust your health to our culinary endeavors. We reached a compromise. I agreed she could bring you food. She promised she would make you eat healthier in the future."

Sandra groaned. "Ida, you have no idea what you have done to me. Margaret makes you look like a cream puff."

Ida gave a gruff grunt. "Good. Somebody needs to make you listen. Since you aren't doing a very good job of taking care of yourself."

"I can take care of myself."

"Sure you can. Let's see how you're doing." Ida flipped open Sandra's chart and began to scan the data.

Sandra wiped her sweaty palms on the sheet as she waited.

"First and foremost, your heart is healthy."

Sandra expelled a sigh of relief.

Ida glanced at her. "It won't be if you don't start taking better care of yourself. A nurse will be in shortly to remove the monitoring equipment, so you can get a good night's rest." She glanced back down at the chart and continued. "Your blood pressure has stabilized, but it's still higher than I would like and you are anemic."

Sandra leaned her head back against the pillows. As long as there was no damage to her heart, she could handle the rest. She would do whatever Ida suggested.

"Now are you ready for the bad news?"

Sandra felt her gut clench. The monitor announced her agitation.

Ida flipped the chart closed and reached over to turn the monitor off. "Don't get upset. You've got several decades left yet. The bad news is you've got to make some changes."

"Okay," Sandra conceded.

"I'm going to release you in the morning. I'll give you a prescription for what amounts to a kick-ass multi-vitamin. Take it for thirty days. I want you to start a daily exercise routine of walking. After you return from your three month hiatus, cut your working hours to no more than fifty hours a week."

Sandra nodded. She would have to think about the fifty-hour work week, but that could wait until later.

Ida frowned. "I thought I'd get more of an argument from you. I guess this little episode gave you a scare."

"More than you can imagine," Sandra admitted.

"Good. Sometimes a bit of a scare can be a healthy thing. Now, don't forget to take the vitamins," Ida said as she turned to leave.

"I will," Sandra promised.

Ida laughed as she headed out the door. "I know you will." She turned just before the door closed and said, "I gave the prescription to Margaret." She walked away before Sandra could respond.

Sandra smiled as she heard Ida's chuckles drifting down the hallway.

After the nurse removed the heart monitor, Sandra fell asleep. She opened her eyes to find Carol sitting by her bed-side.

Anger surged through her as she pushed herself into a sitting position. "Where's your lawyer?"

Carol was nervously twisting the gold chain that served as a handle on her purse. "I apologize for showing up at your office. I only did it because I was so angry with you."

"Angry with me!" Sandra said amazed. "Isn't that supposed to be my line?"

"Oh, Sandra."

Sandra started to say more, but the tears streaming down Carol's cheeks startled her into silence. In their eight years together, Sandra had rarely seen Carol cry.

"I only slept with Ingrid to get even with you. I resented you never having time for me. I just wanted to get your attention."

Sandra sighed. "You certainly achieved your goal."

Carol leapt from the chair and threw herself into Sandra's arms.

"Please. You have to forgive me." She clung to Sandra and sobbed harder.

Sandra sat stiffly, surprised by Carol's outburst. She slowly became aware of the tantalizing smell of Carol's perfume. Carol's hands clutched at her back, pulling her closer crushing her breasts again Sandra. Her tears were warm on Sandra's neck. Sandra's arms encircled Carol and held her tighter.

"I promise. I'll be so much better. You'll see," Carol said as her lips brushed Sandra's neck.

Everything was happening so fast. Her growing feelings of desire took Sandra by surprise. She was grateful the heart monitor was no longer on her; otherwise, it would have been transmitting her desire to everyone within hearing distance. The feelings she had felt for Carol early in their relationship were resurfacing.

"Sandra, I'm so happy. Everything will be just as it was before this horrible thing happened. You can call the bank and tell them there's been a mistake."

Sandra felt as though someone had poured ice water over her.

Carol rushed on. "I'll buy some fabulous new clothes and after you're released we can go away somewhere. Just the two of us. Maybe Hawaii? No. That's too cliché. Hong Kong. Yes. I've always wanted to visit the Orient."

Sandra gently untangled Carol's arms from around her.

"What's wrong?" Carol asked. "Don't you want to go to Hong Kong?"

Sandra stared at Carol, really seeing her for perhaps the first time. Carol would never change. In many ways, she was a child. Sandra tried to summon the disgust and hatred she had felt when she discovered Carol with Ingrid, but it was gone. There was nothing left but sadness and an odd sense of freedom.

Her sadness was for the things Carol would never experience — the sense of satisfaction in creating something, or in doing a job well. The empowerment achieved in knowing you could survive on your own, if you had to, or the sheer joy of loving someone for no other reason than love. Looking at Carol's tear-streaked face, Sandra realized she had never known true love herself. She had fallen in love with the idea of love when she met Carol. She never felt the kind of love you read about in romance novels or see in those wonderful old black and white movies.

I will, she promised herself. *I will find a woman to love. Someone who will love me for who I am, not what I own. And if I don't, I'll never settle for less again.*

She looked at Carol and made her decision. It was impossible for her to hate Carol. Perhaps she should, and maybe she was about to make a mistake, but it was her mistake to make.

"I'll call the bank tomorrow," Sandra said, brushing Carol's hair away from her eyes.

Carol grabbed her and hugged her again. "I knew you would come to your senses."

Sandra extracted herself from Carol's embrace.

"What's wrong?"

"I'll call the bank and make arrangements to have a monthly allowance deposited to your account. But you can't move back."

Carol began to cry again. "But, I promised to change."

"Listen to me. The relationship is over. I have to move on with my life."

Carol stopped crying. A frown creased her forehead. "Is there someone else?"

"No. I've reached a point in my life where I need more." Seeing Carol's confusion, she tried to explain her feelings. "I want the white picket fence."

"You want to get married?" Carol asked, clearly dumbfounded.

Sandra shook her head and smiled. She would never be able to explain her desires to Carol. "I need to be on my own," she said instead.

"But you'll still give me my money?"

Sandra could see Carol was holding her breath.

"Yes. I'll set up a monthly allotment. I'll call Lynda Hopkins and we'll work out an agreement."

Carol smiled and began drying her tears. "Well, don't forget. Since you're throwing me out of the penthouse, I'll need enough money to buy a new one and . . ."

"Carol, don't push your luck."

A look of anger flashed across Carol's face, but for once prudence apparently stopped her tongue.

Long after Carol left, Sandra stared at the ceiling wondering where her new life would lead.

CHAPTER SIX

Sandra breathed a sigh of relief when she stepped through the hospital doors into the warm afternoon sun. Scheduled for release that morning, one bureaucratic delay after another dragged the process out.

"Damn," she groaned when she reached into her purse for her keys. Her car was still in the company parking lot. She considered calling Margaret, but anticipated the lecture that would accompany the trip. She called Allison instead.

While waiting for Allison, she made use of a pay phone in the lobby to make the necessary calls to arrange Carol's monthly allotment. She felt good about the decision to set up the allotment. It was the right thing to do.

With the arrangements made, she went outside and found a quiet corner in the sun to wait.

By the time Allison arrived, rush hour traffic was in full swing. Sandra tried to start a conversation, but Allison seemed preoccupied. They fell silent as the backlog of traffic inched along.

Sandra waited. Allison would talk about whatever was bothering her when she was ready. In the meantime, Sandra filled the silence by asking about Allison's son and mother.

"Brian spends every spare moment of his time surfing the Internet. If time is any indication, he must know everyone online. His grades dropped slightly at the beginning of the school year. I threatened to limit his computer time and they came back up," Allison said.

Sandra smiled to herself. Allison would never take away anything Brian enjoyed doing. The multiple sclerosis was growing steadily worse. He could no longer do many things by himself. "And Mom," Allison continued, "stays busy with her volunteer work. I swear, she works more hours than I do." Allison fell silent, as the traffic grew heavier.

"Is something wrong?" Sandra asked, unable to wait any longer. Allison's restless shifting and throat clearing was beginning to get on her nerves.

"I need to discuss something with you. I feel bad about bringing it up," Allison admitted as she moved to the right-hand lane to avoid the fumes of a city bus inching along in front of them.

"Does it have anything to do with the office?"

Allison nodded.

"The Dunbar project?"

"No." Allison cleared her throat again. "It's not completely work related. Wait a minute," Allison whipped her car into a parking lot and stopped.

"I can't do this and drive at the same time," she said with

a sigh. "I'm sorry to drop this on you, but I think it's important you know what's happened. Gordon fired Charles Carlton yesterday morning."

Sandra started to speak, but Allison stopped her.

"You would have fired him. Gordon told me he warned Charles the boards were unacceptable. That's when Charles went to you with them." She fidgeted with the chain on her watchband. "After being fired, Charles went straight to MacMillan. They hired him."

Sandra leaned her head back against the seat. MacMillan was her biggest competitor. "I assume there's more. I can't see you being this upset over Charles being fired."

Allison nodded. "Charles called all of our major clients and," she hesitated, "told them you are a lesbian. Lisa Allen from Overby's called me this morning. Charles told her you fired him because he disagreed with you over the content of some of our ads. He made it sound like you were opposing ads that, and I quote, 'represented the natural acts between men and women'." Without giving Sandra time to comment, Allison rushed on.

"Roy Landreth from Mega Star Foods called threatening to pull his stores out of the malls. He believes Tate Enterprises misrepresented itself, and you will become a determent to his businesses. To top everything off, someone called the paper. You made the business section." She pulled a newspaper from under the seat and handed it to Sandra.

After reading the article announcing to all of Dallas that she was a lesbian, Sandra tried to evaluate how this would affect business.

"I'm really sorry all this is happening," Allison said. "I know you were ready to get away, but frankly, I'm afraid if you disappear now, it'll look like you're hiding."

"I won't be hiding," Sandra assured her.

"What are you going to do?"

Sandra sat quietly for a minute. "Get a copy of the layouts Charles wanted to use and then contact Molly Devonshire. Ask her if she's interested in printing our side of the story."

Allison grinned. "Sandra, you're evil. You know Molly Devonshire will take one look at those layouts and renew her crusade on pornography in advertising."

"Let's hope by the time she gets through singing our praises for refusing to contribute to *'the degradation of women by mass market money-mongers'* no one will remember I'm a lesbian."

"So it's true?" Allison asked.

Sandra stared at her. "You didn't know?"

"We've never discussed it."

"Does it bother you?" Sandra's fingers tapped a nervous dance on her thigh, while Allison looked out the window. It never occurred to her Allison might not know. However, when she thought about it, why would anyone know?

Carol never attended office events, and Sandra rarely mentioned her. Sandra's business life and her personal life were separate worlds, and she preferred to keep them that way.

"To be honest, I'd have to say at some level I suspected," Allison admitted. "Since all of this happened with Charles, I've wondered why we never talked about your life. We've spent hours talking about my problems with Mom and Brian, but I know next to nothing about your life outside the office," she said and shrugged. "I finally had to admit to myself why I never asked about your life. I think I knew and wasn't comfortable with it." She turned to look at Sandra. "I'm sorry. It was wrong of me."

Sandra nodded and looked away. She was not sure how she felt about being dragged out of the closet. "We'd better get going. Margaret will call out the National Guard if we're later than she thinks we should be."

Allison's chuckle revealed her relief in escaping the current conversation. "I've had a couple of close encounters with Margaret already. I'm not ready for another one."

Allison left after a none-too-subtle hint from Margaret that Sandra needed to rest.

"I'll take care of the things we discussed," Allison promised as she waved good-bye. "I'll make arrangements to get your car home."

After Allison left, Sandra started toward her office.

"And where do you think you're headed?" Margaret demanded.

"I thought I'd spend some time working on the speech I'm giving . . ." Sandra let the sentence drop as Margaret crossed her arms over her massive chest.

"It's rest you'll be needin'. Dr. Ida said you were to take it easy."

Sandra considered protesting, but decided it was useless. Arguing with Margaret was as fruitless as arguing with a wall. She went to her bedroom.

After changing into her pajamas, Sandra crawled into bed. She laughed softly when she found a small bell by the bedside with a note from Margaret instructing her to ring it if she needed anything.

Sandra waited until she was sure Margaret was busy and out of earshot before calling her lawyer, Elizabeth Brubeck. She needed to take care of one more item. After a few quick assurances that she was feeling fine, Sandra dictated the changes she wanted made to her will.

"Sandra, as your attorney I feel obligated to make sure you really want to do this. It's understandable you would want to leave Margaret something. However, half of your estate seems excessive. That's an awful lot of money," Elizabeth stressed.

"Liz, I have no family. It's what I want, right now."

"You know best. You can always change it. By the way," she added, "Rita and I were sorry to hear about you and Carol splitting."

"Thanks. It was best for both of us."

"Don't hesitate to call if there's anything we can do. I'll drop by tomorrow to get your signature on these changes."

After hanging up the telephone, Sandra remembered she had promised to send Carol's passport and birth certificate to Lynda Hopkins. Moving quietly, Sandra slipped into the master bedroom and removed the lock box from the safe. Feeling like a disobedient child, she took the box and scurried back to bed. She stuffed the items in an envelope and placed the envelope in the dresser by the door. Hiding the lock box under the bed, she rang the bell Margaret had left.

"Why aren't you sleepin'?" Margaret demanded as she came into the room.

"I remembered something and couldn't sleep until it was taken care of."

Margaret eyed her suspiciously. Sandra felt a twinge of guilt, but reminded herself she was not actually telling a lie. She couldn't sleep.

"I promised I'd mail a package to Carol's lawyer. I forgot to do it. I believe it's there in the dresser. Could you call a courier and have it delivered today?"

Margaret went to the dresser and found the envelope. "Don't be tryin' this again. I won't be believin' it," she warned sternly, shaking the envelope at Sandra. "Now, to sleep with you."

Suitably chastised, Sandra nodded.

As Sandra suspected, Molly Devonshire wanted the interview. She was practically foaming at the mouth when she left Sandra's penthouse with a copy of the offensive layouts and

Sandra's assurance that Tate Enterprises would never resort to using such sexually explicit advertising.

The paper ran a photo of the layout with a long article on the hidden dangers of this caliber of advertising. Molly wrapped the story up by praising the vast amount of charity work Sandra did for women and children and the contributions made by Tate Enterprises to charities too numerous to mention.

Allison called Sandra an hour after the paper hit the street. Roy Landreth from Mega Star Foods had decided to leave his stores in Tate Enterprises' chain of malls.

Sandra sat on the balcony. Three days out of the hospital and she was already bored beyond belief. Other than her short walks in the morning and late afternoon, she spent most of her time reading or sleeping.

The chest pains and heartburn were gradually dissipating and she was restless. The thought of doing this for three months was almost more than she could stand. She glanced at her watch. Allison had promised to stop by later in the afternoon and give her a brief run-down on what was happening at the office.

Sandra returned to the bedroom. She reached across the bed for the book she was trying to read. As she did so, her toe stubbed something beneath the bed. She knelt down and saw the lock box she had failed to return to the safe after removing Carol's passport and birth certificate.

She pulled the box out and opened it. At the bottom, beneath a small bundle of cash that served as a security blanket for her, and some of Sandra's papers, lay a large manila envelope. It contained practically everything from her father's meager estate.

He had sold the old travel trailer, after she left for college, and moved into a low-rent apartment complex. He took care

77

of the grounds and did minor repair jobs in exchange for his rent. To supplement his income, he hired out for odd jobs around the neighborhood. Sandra tried to give him money, but he always refused it. Her father had always insisted on being paid in cash, which meant he usually worked in low paying jobs. Sandra credited her father's idiosyncrasy to the fact he was a compulsively private person.

Less than two years after she moved back to Dallas, her father was killed when he fell from a roof he was patching. Numb with grief, Sandra made the simple arrangements he would have wanted. Since her father was an only child, and his parents had died before Sandra was born, there was no family to notify.

Sandra donated his meager wardrobe and furniture to Goodwill and paid to have his ancient truck towed away.

At the time of his death, she had been emotionally unable to deal with his private personal effects. She had placed everything in the envelope and stored it in the lock box.

She dumped the contents of the envelope onto the bed and carefully separated them. She found his cracked and peeling wallet, a scarred Barlow pocketknife, and a small envelope containing four photos. She swallowed the burning lump in her throat and removed the photos.

The first one was of her when she was a child. The stamp on the back gave the year and the address of a photo shop in San Antonio. She squinted at the photo. Judging by the date, she had been about four-years-old. She was standing on a porch clutching a scruffy-looking bear. The bear was wearing a plaid vest. An odd-shaped hat sat at a jaunty angle over one ear.

For years, her father kept the photo hidden in a cigar box under his bed. She was about ten when she discovered it while cleaning and had instinctively known not to ask him about it.

There was a shadow of the photographer in the lower left corner. Over time, Sandra started associating the shadow with her mother. During the lonely years of childhood, she developed an intense love/hate relationship with the mysterious shadow. When she left for college, she stole the snapshot to take with her. She felt so guilty she returned it on her first trip home.

Looking at the photo, Sandra again wondered about the mysterious photographer. Was it a shadow of her mother? She turned her attention to the bear she held in the photo. *Mr. Peepers,* she thought suddenly. The name came from her subconscious, along with an unsettling sense of loss. She could not remember when or where the bear had disappeared from her life.

Uneasy with the emotions running through her, she turned her attention to the remaining photographs, which were of her and her father at various times in her life. Sandra studied the awkward-looking child for several minutes before stuffing the photos back in the envelope.

She picked up his battered wallet. The brown imitation leather was cracked and peeling with age. She started to put it back into the envelope. The wallet was the only truly personal thing he had owned. She ran her finger along a cracked seam and slowly opened the wallet. The lump in her throat grew. She coughed trying to ease the discomfort.

The wallet contained eight dollars. The window where a driver's license would normally fit was empty. She searched through the inner pockets looking for his license. There was not one, but in the last pocket, she found a pale blue envelope.

The envelope had been folded several times and was stained and worn with age. She opened it carefully to avoid ripping the fragile paper. The letter addressed to her father had a San Antonio return address, but no name. Curious as to why he would have carried the letter for so many years, she opened it. The letter contained no date.

Dear Vernon,
  I wanted to plead with you one more time to let me see Sandra. I love her dearly and miss my darling girl.

Please, don't let your hatred for me keep our daughter from her mother. Vernon, she is only four. She doesn't understand what's happening. I promise you, she will never know why I left.

I don't have a telephone, but you can contact me at this address or call me at work. My number is below. I'm begging you. Please, don't keep her from me.
Jessica.

Sandra's hands trembled as she read the letter through again. Her mother had wanted to see her and her father refused. Why? Why had he never told her where her mother was? He let her believe her mother did not want to see her. Had her mom changed her mind after writing the letter?

Sandra was still asking herself questions when she heard Margaret and Allison's voices in the hallway. She shoved the items back into the box and pushed it under the bed. She was sitting on the balcony when Allison joined her.

"How are you feeling?" Allison's anxious eyes studied her.

"Fine." She tried to think of something to say, but couldn't think of anything but the lock box. "How's work?" she asked, without any real interest.

Allison began a run-down on what was happening, but Sandra soon tuned her out and again tried to understand why her father had lied to her.

"And the wolf ate them all up!" Allison said loudly.

Sandra blinked. "What wolf?" she stammered.

"You're a million miles away. You should have told me you were too tired for this. You're supposed to be resting." She stood, but Sandra was already lost in her thoughts.

"Sandra." Allison was kneeling before her. "Should I call Ida? You look awfully pale."

"No. I'm fine." She bit her lower lip.

"You don't look fine. You're pale and trembling. Let me help you back inside."

Sandra allowed Allison to lead her from the balcony. She

needed to talk to someone. *Laura*, she thought immediately, and experienced a stab of guilt.

Laura would be upset with her for not calling and letting her know she had been sick. Sandra had thought about calling her, but since she had not actually suffered a heart attack, it seemed somewhat silly. Laura was always so busy.

"Allison, can you drive me somewhere? Margaret won't let me leave alone without a major row."

"Sure, but do you think you should?"

Sandra felt her frustration growing. "I'm not sick. I was tired, and now I'm rested. No, I'm bored out of my mind. I need to get out of this room. I want to go spend a few days with a friend. She lives about an hour from here." Sandra packed a small bag before grimacing. "Now, all I have to do is get past the warden."

Allison laughed. "I don't envy you. She really is very protective of you."

Sandra felt like a child again as she entered the kitchen where Margaret was cleaning the refrigerator.

"I'm going to go spend a couple of days with a friend. Allison is going to drive me." Sandra rushed on as Margaret turned to stare at her. "I'll leave her number on the table for you."

"You're supposed to be restin'," Margaret reminded.

"I can rest at Laura's just as well as I can here. She lives in the country, so I can sit on the porch all day and enjoy the fresh air and sunshine."

"Did you ask Dr. Ida?" Margaret demanded.

Sandra sighed. This was going to be worse than she anticipated.

Allison stepped forward and took Sandra's suitcase. "I'm sorry to rush you, but I promised Mom I'd be home early, so we really do need to be going." She turned to Margaret. "Don't worry. I'll make sure she's settled in before I leave her." Without waiting for Margaret to respond, she pushed Sandra out the door and into the elevator. As the elevator door closed, hiding Margaret's disapproving glare, Sandra pulled a spare car key from the wallet in her purse. "Do you know she actually hid my keys?" she said, taking her suitcase from Allison.

"She's worried about you," Allison said, releasing the bag and resting her hands on the rails around the elevator walls.

"I know, but it gets a little overwhelming sometimes."

"Did you want me to drive your car?" Allison eyed Sandra's keys.

"No. I was afraid you wouldn't be able to lie well enough to get past Margaret," Sandra admitted. Seeing Allison's frown, Sandra moaned. "Don't you start, too. I'm a medical prisoner. I have to get away. I love Margaret dearly, but she's driving me nuts. I swear I feel fine. I'm eating and I sleep at least eight hours a night. I've not experienced any pain since I left the hospital, so please don't start in on me."

"Are you really going to stay with a friend?"

"Yes. She works out of her home most of the time so she'll be there in case I need anything."

Allison shook her head and laughed. "Think of the story this would make. Sandra Tate, sneaking out of the house like a wayward teenager."

Sandra smiled before she replied. "Don't forget who signs your check."

Allison gave a mock salute. "Just make sure you let me know when it's safe for me to come back. I don't want Margaret on my butt."

Sandra returned the salute.

Sandra called Laura from the car. "I'm calling to invite myself over."

"Good. I need someone to test my new casserole."

"As long as it isn't tuna." Sandra detested tuna casserole.

"Would I feed you tuna casserole?"

"I'll be there in less than an hour."

Sandra felt the tension draining away as she drove out of the city. She was actually smiling by the time she pulled into Laura's driveway.

The small, blue cottage sat in a grove of oak trees. After she parked her car, Sandra stood by it and closed her eyes, listening to the wind in the trees. It was such a peaceful sound. She continued to listen until she heard the closing of the front door. She opened her eyes and found Laura watching her from the front steps.

"I sometimes think this place is the closest thing I've ever known to a real home," Sandra said, walking to Laura.

"It's always opened to you, day or night," Laura said. She wrapped her arms around Sandra and held her close.

Sandra clung to her for an extra long moment before they went inside. She sniffed appreciatively at the wonderful aroma. "Umm, that smells good. What is it?"

"I don't have a name for it yet, but it's a combination of chicken and vegetables and a new blend of herbs. You can be my guinea pig. Sit down. It's almost ready."

Sandra sat at the wooden table. "It always amazes me your kitchen is so small," Sandra said, gazing around the compact room. "I'd expect someone who makes their living creating new recipes to have an enormous, professionally stocked kitchen."

"I want to create simple recipes anyone can prepare. I keep my kitchen similar to my mother's. If I can cook it here, then I know anyone can replicate it."

"I wouldn't bet on that," Sandra said, thinking about her own cooking skills. She cooked for her father for years and later for herself, until she hired Margaret, but her efforts were mediocre at best.

"Your problem is you don't like to eat," Laura said. "You don't take the time to understand and enjoy food."

"I eat when I'm hungry," Sandra defended.

"Which is precisely my point. You eat for survival. I enjoy the smell, taste and texture of food."

"You make it sound like sex," Sandra said as Laura bent to remove the casserole.

"Actually, food and sex have a lot in common. They both satisfy a basic human need. We wouldn't survive without them."

"You will not die without sex," Sandra snorted.

"Speak for yourself!" Laura quipped and placed the casserole on the table. "Speaking of such, how is Carol?"

"We've split up," Sandra replied.

Laura stopped and looked at her. "Do you want to talk about it?"

"There's nothing to talk about," Sandra said.

Laura nodded and began to remove plates from the cabinet. Sandra got up to get the silverware.

They ate and discussed the delicious new recipe. Laura made a few notes on changes she wanted to try. She would continue to experiment with the recipe, until she achieved the exact taste she was looking for. They talked about the weather and the local news as they did dishes. Afterwards, they settled on the large, overstuffed couch in the living room with a cup of coffee.

"It's still too cool to sit on the porch at night," Laura stated. "We'll have to make do in here."

Sandra took a sip of the coffee and leaned her head back.

"Are you ready to talk about what brought you out this way?" Laura asked as she curled her feet beneath her.

Sandra pulled the letter from her purse sitting on a table at the end of the couch. "I found this in my father's wallet today." She continued to sip her coffee while Laura read the letter.

Laura went through it slowly. "I've often wondered about your mom," she said, re-folding the letter. "You've never mentioned her except that one time in college when you told me she left when you were a child."

"I told you all I knew." Sandra set her now empty cup on the floor. "Dad wouldn't talk about her. I never knew any other family members who could tell me. According to Dad, my grandparents died when I was young, and he and mom were both from single child homes. There was no one else to ask." She found herself wondering if it was true. Had he lied about that too? Stabbed by guilt, she pushed the thought away. Her father obviously had a good reason for lying to her about her mother.

"You were four when she left?"

Sandra nodded.

"Do you remember anything about her?" Laura asked.

"I think, I recall a trip to the zoo. I may remember laughing with her and her hugging me. But, that may have been a dream or something." Sandra's voice cracked and she coughed to cover it. "I have no memory of her leaving or what she looked like."

Laura held up the letter. "This sounds like she wanted to see you, and your father wouldn't let her."

"Why would he do that?" Sandra leaned toward Laura. "I've spent the entire day wondering what she could have done that was so horrible he felt he had to keep me from seeing her, and for him to lie to me all of those years."

"He must have felt like he had a reason," Laura said.

Sandra pushed her hair away from her face. "I was remembering how we used to move around so much. I can't help but wonder if it was so she wouldn't know where I was."

"It's possible," Laura agreed. They sat quietly for a moment. "What do you plan to do about this?" Laura prompted.

"Nothing. It's too late now."

"Why?"

"I've not seen her in thirty-three years. I'm sure she has

a life with a family. I doubt she'd be too happy to have me show up." Sandra shrugged. "Think about it. I've not exactly spent my adult life as a hermit. She could have found me during the last few years if she wanted to."

"Have you ever thought about trying to find her?"

Sandra rested her head on the back of the couch and stretched out her legs. "I've considered it several times over the years. I even hired a private investigator once, but I chickened out and called it off before he could find anything."

"There's an address on the envelope," Laura observed as she sipped her coffee.

"It's thirty years old. She wouldn't still be there."

"Probably not, but it would be a place to start."

"What if she's remarried? I'd never find her," Sandra argued.

"Go to San Antonio, look around, and check the county records. They will inform you if she's remarried."

Sandra couldn't sit still and kept rearranging her body on the couch. "My problem isn't how to find her," she finally admitted. "It's more a matter of whether I want to. And even if I did, would she want to be found."

Laura groaned, "Sandra, you are my burden in life." She held out her arms. Sandra scooted around and sat between her legs with her back resting against Laura's body. Laura wrapped her arms around her. "You make life so complicated," she admonished as Sandra examined Laura's hands.

"I can't just act, the way you do," Sandra justified.

"I know. You have to analyze everything to death. Have you ever done one spontaneous thing in your life?"

Sandra had a sudden vision of Lona's tangled black hair between her thighs and felt a light sweat break out along her collar.

"I didn't think so," Laura chided, taking Sandra's silence as an admission of guilt. "Can I ask you something?"

"Sure, but you probably already know the answer, since you know everything."

Laura playfully punched her arm. "Why didn't you bring Carol with you when you would come to visit me?"

"You mean besides the fact you two disliked each other instantly?"

"I didn't necessarily dislike her. I just felt you two weren't exactly compatible."

Sandra remained quiet for a moment. There was more to her keeping Carol and Laura separated, but how could she explain?

"It's so complicated," she began. "I didn't want you to know me in that part of my life. I think I was ashamed."

"Of me?" Laura's voice sounded hurt.

"No, of myself. I was ashamed of the person I became when I was with Carol. Maybe I was even ashamed of Carol, and the way she treated people. I didn't want any of that world to contaminate this one."

Laura seemed to hesitate. "No one called me when you were hospitalized. I read about it in Molly Devonshire's article. It scared me. I didn't feel comfortable calling you. I don't even know if you're all right now."

Sandra turned to find tears in Laura's eyes. "I'm sorry. I'm fine. It was only an anxiety attack. The doctor says all I need to do is rest." Sandra wiped a tear from Laura's cheek. "I'm so sorry. I thought about calling you," she said lamely. "It's not right for me to just show up when I need someone to help put me back together, or get me back on the right track. I shouldn't do that to you." She wiped another tear away. "I really am sorry. Would you like to go home with me? I could introduce you to Margaret."

Laura laughed. "From everything you've told me about Margaret, I'm not sure I'm ready for her. Maybe you could list me in your Rolodex as someone to notify in case of an emergency."

"I have a better idea," Sandra joked. "Why don't I leave half of Tate Enterprises to you instead? And then, if I die, they'll be sure to notify you."

Laura laughed again and sniffed. "Would it provide me with enough money to give up my consultant work and concentrate full time on creating new recipes?"

"Not with the way you buy groceries."

Sandra did not tell Laura that she had, in fact, named her as beneficiary for half of Tate Enterprises, or that at present value, the company's worth amounted to more than Laura could spend in three lifetimes.

"Can I spend the night?" Sandra asked to change the subject.

"Only if you brought your own toothbrush."

Later that night, they lay curled together in Laura's only bed. Laura yawned loudly. "Why do you think we never became lovers? We're best friends, and we've done everything else together."

"Because you insist on being straight and I'm not a man," Sandra said as she closed her eyes.

"Oh, yeah," Laura mumbled sleepily. "Do you remember the wild dream you had when I first met you?"

"Which one? Becoming President of the United States or marrying Mrs. Peal and living happily ever after?"

"Neither. The one about buying a motorcycle and riding all over the country."

They both drifted off to sleep.

CHAPTER SEVEN

Sandra sat in bed, twisting the gold ring off and on her finger, as she watched a flock of sparrows invade the birdfeeder. Her thoughts were too ridiculous to put into words. Margaret would surely have her committed. What would Laura think? She gazed at her best friend's face, now softened with sleep.

She recalled Laura's question of the previous night. For a moment, she indulged in a fantasy. What would it be like to wake up beside Laura every morning? She glanced around the sparsely decorated room. They would probably be able to live together peacefully, and Sandra did love her. *As one loves a sister*, she mused. Laura would be an amiable partner, but Sandra needed more. She wanted a relationship with passion.

Before she could settle into a relationship, she had to find out who she was. She squirmed with impatience; she wanted answers. She never liked questions in her life, but had carried one around with her for as long as she could remember. Maybe it was time to find the woman who gave her life and ask her why she abandoned her child.

"Sandra," Laura moaned in a voice heavy with sleep. "I'm not a morning person, in case you've forgotten. Please, tell me why you're sitting in the middle of my bed at the crack of dawn, huffing and puffing like a marathon runner."

"Did I wake you?" Sandra teased. Laura's bark was much worse than her bite.

"No, *mija*. I always wake up before the sun comes up. It gives me time to feed the chickens and milk the cows."

Sandra snorted. "You wouldn't know which end of a cow to milk."

"Oh, and I suppose you would?" Laura gave up the pretense of sleep and propped her back against the headboard.

"No, but since milk comes from a female cow, I bet I could figure it out faster than you."

Laura grimaced. "If you are going to be crude, I'm going to shower. Then, I'll fix breakfast."

"I have a better idea," Sandra said, beginning to fidget.

"What?" A look of mock horror crossed Laura's face. "Oh, no. Please tell me you aren't going to suggest you cook breakfast?"

Sandra stuck out her tongue. "Let's go in to the city. I'll buy you breakfast, and we'll go shopping."

"Shopping! You? You hate shopping," Laura exclaimed. "You're the person who used to do my math homework for a whole semester just so I'd go once a year to buy you a couple of shirts and a pair of jeans."

Sandra crawled off the bed. "I wasn't thinking about shopping for clothes."

Laura frowned. "What do you want to shop for?"

"Promise you won't laugh."

"Okay, I promise."

"A motorcycle."

Laura's mouth fell open. She stared at Sandra for several seconds before speaking. "Are you serious?"

Sandra smiled and nodded.

"You're really going to do it?"

Sandra kept nodding. "After talking to you last night, I got to thinking about the dream I had of buying a motorcycle and driving off into the sunset." She shrugged. "I'm not interested in driving off into the sunset anymore, but I have a lot of free time to fill before going back to work. I think maybe it's time I had some fun."

"You're really, really going to do it!" Laura shrieked, leaping over and grabbing Sandra in a bear hug. "Damn, Tater, I've waited twenty years for you to loosen up and do something wild. I knew you had it in you."

Sandra grinned as Laura pulled her from the bed and danced her around the room.

"It's been about that long since I let anyone get away with calling me Tater," Sandra said.

"Come on," Laura urged. "Let's skip breakfast and go buy it before you change your mind."

"Don't you think we should pick up some literature first?" Sandra hedged.

"Agghh!" Laura shook her. "Just once, Tater, go with your gut instinct and do something just for the sake of wanting it. You're filthy rich. If the damn thing breaks, buy another one."

They moved apart. Sandra picked up her shoes. "All right, Ms. Spontaneity. Let's go. I'll buy the first bike I see that I like," Sandra promised as she pulled on her shirt. She stopped fiddling with her collar and looked at Laura frowning. "Should we stick to brand names?" she asked and ducked as Laura threw a pillow at her.

They were at their eighth dealership, Dee's Bike and Repair Shop. Laura spied the small, unassuming place as they drove along the interstate. Sandra and Laura walked into the showroom, which paled in comparison to the previous dealerships they had visited. Sandra was about to suggest they go elsewhere when she saw the bike. It was red and white with an abundance of gleaming chrome. "That's it," she breathed in awe.

Laura turned to where Sandra was pointing. "Isn't it kind of big?"

A tall, muscular woman with short black hair approached them. "Good morning. I'm Dee Salazar," she said, beaming what Sandra now thought of as a dealership smile. "What can I show you today?" Her gaze slid over Laura.

"Are you the owner?" Sandra asked, reading the hand-painted sign on the far wall. Dee nodded proudly.

"She's interested in the red and white one over there," Laura broke in.

"Great choice. That's a 1997 Honda Valkyrie. Come on. Take a closer look." Dee's hand touched Laura's arm briefly as she steered them to the bike.

Sandra saw the gesture and suppressed a smile as Dee began her spiel.

"She's like brand new. She has six cylinders, six carburetors, and hot cams. If you're going to be doing any driving through neighborhoods, you'll really appreciate the quiet shaft-drive and tuned six-into-six exhaust. She has a close-ratio five-speed transmission, maintenance-free hydraulic clutch, electronic ignition, massive 45mm inverted fork, adjustable dual rear shocks, large-section radial tires, triple disc brakes and she rides like a dream."

Sandra walked around the bike, ignoring Dee's list of specifications. She was already in love. She didn't care about carburetors or performance. She didn't even glance at the price tag Dee tried to show her. She was already imagining what it would be like to be astride this beauty on the open road. Dee and Laura were talking, but Sandra ignored them. It had taken her six months to select her Jag. She read dozens of specification brochures and went to three different dealerships before buying it. Today her heart was buying this Honda.

"I'll take it," Sandra said, interrupting an astonished Dee in mid-sentence.

"Ah, great," Dee stuttered. "Would you like to take it out for a spin first?"

Sandra shook her head. "I can't drive it, and besides I don't have a license."

Dee rubbed her chin and then slid a hand through her hair. "Maybe you should start with something smaller, lighter. We have a . . ."

"I want this one," Sandra interrupted again.

"Can you ride?" Dee asked Laura.

"Only if it comes with a saddle, four legs and knows the meaning of whoa," Laura assured her.

Sandra could tell Dee was having a problem. "What's wrong?" she asked.

"Well," Dee said, looking up as the door to the shop opened. A short, thin woman waved as she came in. Dee waved back. "My mechanic," she explained. "We do repair work also."

Sandra sensed Dee was stalling. "The bike," she prompted.

"It's sort of complicated." Dee put her hand into her jacket pocket and pulled out a handful of candy. "I'm trying to stop smoking," she explained, and offered them a piece of candy.

As they unwrapped the sweets, Dee continued. "Motorcycles have really come under a lot of governmental scrutiny during the last few years. Some people believe they're too dangerous to be on the road and," she glanced at Sandra, "without the proper caution and equipment, they can be." She motioned around the showroom. "We take our commitment to the safety of our customers seriously. So before you buy this Honda, I think you should learn to ride on something smaller, easier to handle."

"I've already been to eight dealerships and no one mentioned what I should buy," Sandra said, curious as to why this woman would jeopardize a sure sale.

Dee took a deep breath and straightened her shoulders. "I have to live with my conscience. If I sell you this bike knowing it's unsuitable for you and you get yourself killed, I'd have to live with that. If you want something like this," she patted the bike, "you'll have to go somewhere else. I won't sell to you."

Sandra stared at her in amazement and said, "You'd lose a sale for," she looked at the price tag and whistled softly, "this kind of money, on a principle?"

Dee crunched the candy harshly. "As bad as it hurts, yeah I guess I would."

Sandra looked around at the small tidy showroom. "You'll never grow beyond this, with sales practices like that."

Dee looked offended. "Maybe not, but I'll still be able to face myself each morning. Good-bye." She shook their hands and started off.

Devastated, Sandra stared down at the beautiful bike.

Laura shook Sandra's arm and hissed. "Do something. You want this one. Spontaneity Tater!"

"Teach me to ride it," Sandra called after Dee.

Dee stopped and turned, shaking her head. "Sorry. The bike's too much for a beginner."

"I'll buy whatever you tell me I need. You have two weeks to teach me to ride and then you sell me this bike."

Dee walked back to them frowning. "You can buy a bike similar to this one in a dozen places around the city. What's with you?"

"I want this one," Sandra insisted.

Dee's eyebrows rose. She smiled coyly. "And are you accustomed to getting everything you want?"

Sandra looked at the bike and shrugged before turning back to Dee. "I'm not sure I ever wanted anything this badly before."

They stood staring at each other for a long minute while Sandra barely breathed. She wanted this bike. Dee had to sell it to her.

"Here's what I'll do," Dee said at last. "I'll teach you to ride. We have some smaller, used bikes that will be great to start with. I'll give you a list of equipment you'll need — a helmet, some safety pads, etc. You buy those. I'll give you the name of a great shop."

Sandra glanced around, wondering why Dee didn't sell the safety equipment.

As if sensing her thoughts, Dee began to explain. "I don't carry accessories for the rider. There's too much overhead involved with the different clothing sizes. I prefer to specialize in customized bikes, so I stock accessories for the bikes themselves." Dee waved her hand as if to dismiss the sidetracked conversation. "Anyway, back to our deal," Dee said. "I'll teach you everything I can in two weeks. There's a vacant lot behind the shop where you can practice. You'll have to practice riding a lot on your own time, but I'll make sure there's a bike available for you to use. And then, if you pass your driver's test and can convince me that you're capable of handling this bike, I'll sell it to you."

"What happens if I don't convince you?" Sandra asked.

Dee shook her head. "You'll have to go somewhere else."

"What about payment for the lessons?" The businesswoman in Sandra was emerging. She didn't want any loose ends that might cost her the bike.

Dee pulled out her stash of candy and offered it again. "At the end of two weeks, I'll give you the name of my favorite charity and you make a donation in any amount you feel adequate for what you've learned."

Sandra held out her hand. "When can we start?"

"As soon as you get the safety gear."

"Give us a list," Laura said, practically jumping up and down.

Sandra and Laura found the items on Dee's list at the recommended store. With the back seat full of packages, Sandra drove Laura home.

"Stay with me for the next two weeks," Laura prompted as she got out of the Jag and leaned through the window. "It'll be closer to your lessons and I have a feeling." She stopped and looked away.

"What?" Seeing the look on Laura's face, Sandra moaned. "You're not about to get morbid and psychic on me, are you?"

"No. I'm not worried about you dying or anything, but I think things will change." Her gaze held Sandra's. "I don't think you'll ever need me the way you have in the past."

Sandra turned the ignition off and got out of the car. Laura met her halfway around it. "You're the best friend I've ever had," Sandra said, taking Laura's hands. "I'll always need you."

Laura hugged her tightly, before she pulled back to kiss her. Rather than the friendly kiss Sandra expected, their lips held and tentatively explored. Sandra pulled her closer and the kiss lingered. They pulled back and stood staring at each other searching. Suddenly, they both burst into laughter.

Laura extended her hand and Sandra playfully shook it. "We're doomed to friendship for life," Laura said.

"That's me," Sandra sighed in mock severity. "Always the friend, never the lover."

"No dramatics, Tater. That kiss didn't exactly knock your socks off."

Sandra shrugged. "True," she admitted.

"So, will you stay or not?" Laura asked.

"I'll have to pick up some more clothes and let Margaret know how to reach me, but I'll be back tonight."

"I'll fix us something delicious and healthy for dinner. We've got to get you in top form," Laura called, as Sandra climbed into the Jag and started the motor.

CHAPTER EIGHT

Getting away from Margaret proved much easier than Sandra had anticipated. She simply told Margaret she would be spending two weeks with Laura, who was an old college friend and left Laura's telephone number. Not until she was halfway across the city did she realize that Margaret probably thought she was having an affair. She mentally pictured the bike and said, "Maybe I am."

Anxious to get started with her lessons, Sandra headed back to Dee's. She made one quick stop, at the Department of Motor Vehicles, to pick up a study guide for a motorcycle license.

She pulled her Jag around to the side of Dee's shop and went in with the items Dee insisted she buy.

"You came back," Dee called, when Sandra walked in.

"You're going to think I'm a permanent fixture before you get rid of me," Sandra hollered back.

"Can I ask you a question?" Dee asked as they walked into her tiny office.

"Sure."

"Why do you want that bike so bad?" She hesitated. "I don't mean to be rude or anything, but you don't look like the bike type."

Sandra's eyebrows arched. "And what is the bike type?"

"Touché," Dee replied, and sat down at her desk. She motioned to Sandra to take a seat on the couch next to the desk. "Is the bike for weekend recreation, general driving or what?"

Sandra sat and stretched out her legs. "I plan to travel on it."

"Cross-country?" Dee's interest peaked.

"I don't have a particular destination, I'm just going to go."

A look close to jealousy crossed Dee's face. "Dang, that would be great. How long do you plan to do this?"

"A month, maybe two."

Dee seemed to consider Sandra's response. "How are your mechanical skills?"

"I can pump gas, and I've been known to add oil to a car on an occasion or two."

"Ever changed it?"

"No."

"Can you change a tire?"

"No," Sandra answered, starting to feel inadequate.

"Come on." They left the office and walked through the showroom to the garage.

"Connie." The short, thin woman, who had waved at them earlier, turned from a bike she was repairing. "This is Sandra. She's going to be coming in for riding lessons for the next couple of weeks."

Sandra noticed the blank look Connie gave Dee.

Dee continued without explaining. "She's planning on doing some traveling on her new bike, the Honda Valkyrie, and she needs some basic mechanical know-how. Could you spend, oh, say an hour a day, giving some basic pointers? You know. Minor emergency things she might encounter on the road."

"Dee?" Connie began.

Dee held up her hands and stopped her. "We've worked it all out. I'll explain later. Can you spare her an hour a day for the next two week?"

"Sure. I can show her as I work."

"Great. She's all yours for an hour." Dee slapped them each on the shoulder and left.

Connie assessed Sandra's clean slacks and silk shirt. "Why don't you watch today and wear something old tomorrow?"

Eager to begin, Sandra nodded.

For the next hour, Connie explained the basic operations of a motorcycle as she continued to work on the carburetor she was rebuilding.

Sandra listened and watched with an intensity she'd never shown for any other lecture.

Connie answered Sandra's questions with quick easy assurance. Before Sandra realized it, Dee was back waiting for her.

"Ready for your first ride?" Dee asked.

Sandra felt her mouth go dry. She could only nod.

"Well, come on." Dee tossed her the helmet Sandra had purchased earlier.

Sandra caught it and turned to Connie. "Thanks, Connie. See you tomorrow." Connie nodded and waved.

Dee led the way to the front of the building. Sandra's breath caught at the sight of what she already considered her bike sitting there.

"I figured you should know what you're working toward. It might give you an extra bit of incentive to get you through the rough spots and sore muscles," Dee said.

Sandra pulled on the helmet as Dee threw a long leg over the leather seat.

"Hop on," Dee instructed as she patted the seat behind her.

Sandra trembled with excitement as she slid her leg over the seat and settled behind Dee.

"Hang on to me and don't make any sudden moves," Dee said. "Let your body become a part of the machine and move with it. Ready?"

"Yes!" Sandra's heart pounded so hard, she wondered if she might be having another attack. *God*, she thought when the powerful motor roared to life. *If dying feels like this, take me now!*

Dee took them through a maze of side streets until they reached IH-35. She headed south, and as the city traffic fell away, she opened-up the throttle. Sandra Tate fell head over heels in love with the powerful machine between her legs. She turned her face to the warm afternoon sun, wishing she could rip the helmet from her head. She wanted to feel the wind in her face and hair, but she knew Dee would not approve, so she closed her eyes and held onto Dee, scarcely breathing. She wanted to absorb every nuance of this moment. She needed to be able to recall every detail. These memories would sustain her until she could ride this beauty by herself.

Sandra almost cried in disappointment an hour later when they rolled back into the parking lot of Dee's shop.

"What do you think?" Dee asked as she got off and removed her helmet.

Sandra took her helmet off and smiled brightly. "After that ride I think I need a cigarette."

Dee laughed loudly. "It's a thrill all right, but I wouldn't say it was better than sex."

It's better than any sex I've ever had, Sandra thought, her body still throbbing with the sensations of the bike.

"So, we'll see you tomorrow morning then?"

Sandra nodded and reluctantly climbed off.

* * * * *

The next two weeks were rougher than Sandra could have ever imagined. Dee started Sandra off with a small scooter. If Dee was satisfied with Sandra's performance each afternoon, Sandra would find a larger, heavier bike waiting for her the next day. Unfortunately, Dee was never satisfied with Sandra just being able to keep the bike upright and going. She insisted Sandra learn how to perform a wild series of slides and maneuvers through an obstacle course of cans and boxes she and Connie created in the lot behind the shop. Dee gave Sandra a key to the shop. Sandra practiced from early morning until she was too exhausted to pick up the bike.

"Try it again," Dee called when Sandra failed for the fifth time to negotiate the course. Sandra struggled to lift the heavy bike. This morning Sandra had found a much heavier bike waiting for her. Its weight and more powerful motor were giving her trouble.

Exhausted, Sandra wondered what Dee's obsession was. She had nothing to gain by Sandra's failure to ride. *Unless she gets her thrills watching me make a fool of myself*, she grumbled to herself.

"Anytime today, Sandra," Dee yelled.

"Fuck off," Sandra snapped as she used her sleeve to wipe the sweat from her eyes.

Without warning, Dee was in front of her. "Listen to me." Her face was red with anger as she jabbed Sandra's shoulder with her finger. "This isn't some toy you can take out and play with. Do you have any idea how many people die on bikes every year? They die because they don't know how to ride, or they're careless or because some moron in a car doesn't take the time to look for them. You've got one more day to successfully negotiate this course. If you can't do it by one o'clock tomorrow, our deal's off. Do you understand that?"

"What the hell's your problem? Why do I need to know how to slide and all this stuff anyway?"

Dee spun on her heels and stormed away. A moment later, Sandra heard the bike that Dee rode roar to life and speed away.

Sandra walked the bike back to the door where Connie stood watching her. "Connie, what's with her? Why should she care whether I can do all those slides or not?"

Connie pulled a cigarette from her pocket and lit it with a match. She leaned against the doorframe and carefully blew out the match. "If I tell you, can you keep your mouth shut?"

"Sure."

"Three years ago, Dee sold a bike to a woman who didn't know much about riding. The woman had a license, and had even owned a bike, but she bought a bike bigger than she could handle. Four days later, a gravel truck pulled out in front of her. She panicked and tried to stop too fast. She lost control and was thrown from the bike. She died the next day. If she could have maneuvered the bike into the slide Dee's been showing you, she'd probably still be alive."

Sandra nodded. "I can understand her feeling bad, but it was ultimately the woman's choice to buy the bike. Dee shouldn't feel guilty about selling it to her."

"The woman was her kid sister." Connie pushed her cigarette into a can of sand that sat by the door. "What she's trying to show you could save your life." Connie turned and went back to her workbench.

Sandra crawled back onto the bike and started it. She was still practicing two hours later when Connie yelled to tell her it was time to stop for the day. She had not been able to complete the course even at a slow cruise.

"I want to stay and work a while longer."

"No. You're already exhausted. Go home and get a good night's sleep. It'll be here in the morning."

"Tomorrow's my last day," Sandra protested. "If I don't get it right by one o'clock, she won't sell me the bike."

"Why is that particular bike so important to you? There are hundreds of bikes on the market."

How could she explain to Connie that she had fallen in love with the Valkyrie? That riding it had made her feel alive. She shifted uncomfortably. "I don't think I can explain."

Connie continued to watch her before nodding. "Never mind, I think I understand. Bring the bike on in and go home. You'll be fine tomorrow. You have the necessary skills. You just need to loosen up and relax."

"Will Dee be all right?" She had not come back to the shop.

"Yeah. She called earlier to check on you." Connie grinned and said, "Personally, I think you both need to loosen up."

CHAPTER NINE

Sandra and Laura sat on the porch enjoying the warm southern breeze. An easy silence settled between them. The distant chirps of crickets and an occasional snuffling from Laura's three horses, in the corral behind the cottage, added to the night's charm.

"I could get used to this," Sandra said, stretching her legs out in front of her to gently push the swing.

"I'm going to miss you when you leave," Laura said.

"Liar. You know you're already longing for peace and quiet."

"I won't miss you bouncing around the house at six-thirty in the morning," Laura admitted and smacked Sandra's leg.

"Do you ever think of getting married again?" Sandra asked, studying Laura's profile in the semi-darkness.

"No. I don't think I will. Marriage is too complicated. Women end up giving up more than men and at this point in my life I'm not willing to give up anything."

"Not even for Mr. Right?"

"Mr. Right is a fairy tale. He fits in right between the Easter Bunny and Santa Claus." Laura hesitated. "If I could find a person who truly loved me and would respect my dreams, I might consider dating. But until someone can kiss me and knock my socks off, I'll remain single."

"I don't think I've ever had my socks knocked off," Sandra said with a frown. "I must be doing something wrong."

"It's probably not what you're doing as much as who you're doing it with. You've just never met the right woman." Laura's voice took on a mock sultry purr. "Just wait, darling, until you ride into town on that beautiful beast of yours. Women will trample each other to get to you."

Sandra's shoulders slumped. "At the rate I'm going I'll probably run over them."

Laura laughed and rumpled Sandra's hair. "That's not the way to knock their socks off."

The following morning Sandra woke to the soft pattering of rain on the window. "Oh, no," she cried and scrambled up to stare out the window.

"What's wrong?" Laura grumbled, still half asleep.

"It's raining!"

"Good. We need rain."

"Not today," Sandra moaned and fell back on the bed. "The obstacle course will be twice as difficult in the rain."

"So reschedule." Laura turned onto her side and pulled a pillow over her head.

Sandra laughed out loud. *Of course. Why hadn't she*

thought of that? She would call Dee and cancel today's ride. They could reschedule it for next week. She would have to wait a few more days before she got her bike, but it gave her more time to practice, and it delayed the chance of failure.

Sandra waited until seven to call Dee at the shop. She was practically dancing with relief as she filled Dee in on the new plan.

"No way," Dee announced, bursting Sandra's bubble. "At some point you'll have to ride in the rain. So you may as well get used to it. This will be good practice for you."

"Wait a minute."

"A deal's a deal, Sandra. If you can't handle the course, you don't need the bike. I have to pick up some parts for Connie and make a delivery, so I'll see you at one sharp." Dee hung up before Sandra could protest further.

"Damn!" She slammed the phone down.

"I take it she didn't buy the delay tactic."

"No. Laura, I don't think I can do it."

Laura tied her robe tighter and yawned. "Well, you won't if you keep thinking like that."

"You don't understand. Dee has me practicing these impossible slides and weaving in and out between paint buckets. It's not like I'll be riding in an AMA Superbike Competition. The entire thing is ridiculous and it's too hard."

Laura spun toward Sandra, her fists settling on her hips. "Sandra Tate, what is wrong with you? I've never known you to be such a whiner. Life is hard. You are facing what most of us face daily. Your architectural ability is a gift granted to only a handful of people. You've never had to struggle for every accomplishment."

"I work hard," Sandra retorted.

"You work long and stressful hours. I'm not trying to diminish your accomplishments. I'm saying you've never known what it's like to sit down and have the design of a building totally elude you. To look at something and have no idea what to do with it."

107

Sandra hesitated. She wanted to lash out at Laura's accusations, but she knew it was true. Designing had never seemed like work to her. Her abilities were a gift.

Sandra gave Laura a sheepish smile, "What are you so discreetly trying to tell me?"

Laura laughed and pulled Sandra into a hug. "Stop whining. Go ride Dee's damn motorcycle or forget about it. It's not worth all of the stress it's creating. There's plenty of other things to worry about."

"Like what?" Sandra asked pulling away.

"Like what your crazy friend is going to do if she doesn't have her coffee very, very soon." Laura headed toward the kitchen. "Go get showered and dressed. I want you out of my hair today. I've got work to do and you're going to be a pain-in-the-butt until this thing is over with."

Sandra started for the bedroom when Laura's voice stopped her.

"Sandra, the motorcycle was supposed to be fun and it's turning into more stress. Maybe this isn't for you. Perhaps you should try something else, or even a smaller bike. Dee has a cute little yellow scooter for sale."

Sandra rolled her eyes. "A yellow scooter is not what I had in mind."

Laura gave her a smug grin. "Well, if that's all you can handle . . ." She let the sentence trail with an elaborate shrug.

"I'll show you what I can handle."

Sandra spent two hours driving around the city looking at past projects. The morning slipped away quickly and took her anxiety with it. Laura was right. The bike was supposed to be fun. She had let her need to excel in everything cloud the enjoyment of learning to ride. She was ready to face the obstacle course. If she failed, the world would not come to a halt. She would simply keep trying until she was able to meet Dee's demands.

She glanced at her watch; three hours remained before she had to meet Dee. She knew what she needed to do. She called her secretary, Betty, with the request.

An hour later, Sandra was headed for the Department of Motor Vehicles where a rental agency was meeting her with a bike. As she pulled into the parking lot of the DMV the rain stopped.

"There you are," Dee called as Sandra came in. "I thought you had changed your mind."

Sandra walked up to her and handed her a blank check.

"What's this?"

"The check that's going to pay for my Honda Valkyrie."

"Even if you manage to complete the obstacle course, you still have to get your license before you can drive it."

Sandra pulled out a slip of paper and handed it to her. "Passed the test an hour ago."

Connie stood in the doorway chuckling.

Dee looked at Sandra and smiled. "All right. Let's see what you can do." She went out to arrange the cans on the obstacle course that the storm had blown over.

Connie rolled one of the used bikes out and stood waiting. "You can do it," she whispered as Sandra pulled on her helmet. "Remember. Loosen up. Pretend the machine's a beautiful woman and you're making love to her for the first time."

Sandra raised the helmet visor and stared at Connie. "What makes you think I make love to women?" She was unable to keep the smile off her face.

Connie blushed, but grinned back. "I can always tell by the way a woman rides whether she's gay or not. And darlin', you got the ride."

"I'm ready anytime you are," Dee called from the far end of the lot.

Groaning, Sandra swung her leg over the seat and started the bike. She dropped the visor over her face.

"Make a slow practice run through," Dee yelled to her. "It'll give you a chance to get a feel for the wet ground."

Sandra rolled her shoulders to relax them and tried to block everything but the machine between her legs and the course in front of her. She maneuvered the bike through the course at a slow speed before making a wide circle at the end of the field to pick up speed. Opening the throttle, she roared back onto the course. Obstacles flashed around her as she zoomed between and around them. The engine hummed and she felt the almost physical merging of her mind and body with the bike. They moved as one. The last obstacle whipped by. She slid the bike into a mud-slinging stop before the garage door.

Sandra raised the helmet visor unable to believe she had completed the course at a high speed, without falling. Connie became her one-person cheering squad, yelling and pounding Sandra on the back.

Dee was running from the back of the lot. Sandra stepped from the bike and released the stand just as Dee picked her up and whirled her around.

"You did it!" Dee shouted as she sat her down and reached into her coat pocket. "Your keys," she said proudly.

Sandra reached for the keys and held them in her palm, staring at them. "Why were they in your pocket? I thought you already decided I couldn't do it."

"No. You decided you couldn't. They were in my pocket because I figured you'd want to take the lady for a ride," she said proudly as she pointed.

Sandra turned to find Connie pushing the Valkyrie out.

"When you get back we'll fill out the paperwork," Dee said and patted Sandra's shoulder. "Be back by five. I have a dinner date. I don't want to be late."

Sandra climbed on and inserted the key. Suddenly she was terrified. "It's always a little scary the first time," Connie said, winking at her. "Just remember what I told you."

"But I'm a terrible lover."

Connie shook her head. "It's physically impossible for a woman to be a bad lover if she's interested in what she's doing."

Maybe that was it, Sandra reasoned as she rode out and merged with traffic. *Maybe sex just hadn't interested her in a long time.*

Sandra dropped by Laura's to pick her up. They rode for over an hour before returning to Laura's cottage.

"Thank you for sharing that with me," Laura called over the engine's idle. "Are you coming back tonight?"

Sandra took off her helmet and ran her hands through her hair. "No. I've got a lot of things I need to do before I leave, but I'll be by before I go. I'll call you tomorrow." They shared a long hug before Sandra put her helmet on and headed back to the shop.

CHAPTER TEN

Connie had left for the day by the time Dee and Sandra completed the paperwork for the sale of the motorcycle.

"I hope I didn't make you late for your dinner engagement," Sandra said as she stood to leave. She felt a twinge of regret over her lessons ending. She would miss Dee and Connie.

"Actually, I haven't asked her yet," Dee replied and stood up.

Sandra glanced at her watch. "It's getting late. Don't you think you should?"

"Yeah, you're probably right. Would you have dinner with me?"

"Me!"

"Yeah. I didn't want to ask you earlier."

Sandra's eyebrows rose. "Afraid I'd turn you down if I didn't make it?"

"No. I knew you would succeed. You wanted it too badly to fail. Nothing was going to stop you."

"Then why didn't you ask?"

Dee cleared her throat and searched her pockets for a piece of candy. "I recognized you the day you came in. I actually met you three or four years ago at a dedication ceremony for the new wing you designed for the children's hospital. I do volunteer work there two nights a week." She handed Sandra a piece of candy. "I wanted to ask you out, but I figured someone like you wouldn't be interested in going to dinner with someone like me. I didn't want to mess things up before you got your bike."

Sandra was torn between hurt and anger. "You thought I wouldn't go to dinner with you because I have more money than you?"

Dee nodded.

"I won't go out with you," Sandra snapped. "But it has nothing to do with money."

"Then why?" Dee asked, visibly hurt and puzzled.

"I thought you taught me to ride because you cared and we were friends, but you never saw beyond the money." She stepped toward Dee. "You're the worse kind of hypocrite. You assumed my money makes me too stuck-up to want to spend time with anyone who had less, when all the time you were wheedling to get the very money you judged me for."

"You're so full of shit," Dee hissed as she leaned closer to Sandra. "Would you have paid any attention to me if I had strolled into your downtown office? Hell, did you pay any attention to me during the past two weeks? Did you even notice me?"

"Yes, I did!"

They stood facing each other. Sandra was as shocked by her admission as Dee appeared to be. The hair on Sandra's arms began to rise as though charged with static electricity. Goosebumps raced down her back only to reverse their course and scramble back up to the nape of her neck. Dee's arms closed around Sandra and pulled her closer. Their lips came together in a frantic need.

"I'm not looking for a relationship," Sandra managed to mutter around kisses as she pulled Dee's coat off her shoulders.

"Neither am I," Dee gasped, shoving the shirt off Sandra's shoulders.

Sandra's body became a center of sensations. Dee's mouth and hands were everywhere, touching her, bringing an almost unbearable hunger to her. Dee's kisses worked a path down Sandra's body as she slipped Sandra's pants off her hips and eased them to the floor.

Sandra kicked the pants off. Her hands explored Dee's body with a hunger she had never known. A wave of desire so intense it shook her gave Sandra the courage to move Dee toward the couch where she pushed her down into a sitting position. She straddled Dee's lap and braced her arms on either side of Dee's head. She shuddered as Dee brushed her fingertips up the inside of her thighs. Their lips met repeatedly. Their tongues probed. Each demanding more access.

Sandra groaned as Dee slipped an arm around her waist and pulled her down onto the fingers of her other hand. Sandra used her legs and the pressure from Dee's arm to push Dee's fingers deeper. She rode Dee's hand, as their kiss grew more intense. Nothing in her previous experience with Carol prepared Sandra for the sensations consuming her.

Unable to remain silent, Sandra threw her head back and screamed Dee's name as Dee's hand brought her to climax. She continued to ride Dee's fingers, enjoying the final ripples of pleasure they offered.

Sandra leaned forward, took one of Dee's ample breasts in

her hands, and teased the hard nipple between her fingertips. "I want to taste you," she whispered in Dee's ear. She moved down until her mouth replaced her fingers on the nipple. She took her time, allowing her tongue to discover every small crevice and contour of the nipple.

Dee's moans filled Sandra with an overwhelming sense of power. Over the years she had stood in countless boardrooms, directed hundreds of employees, raised skyscrapers from weed-choked lots, but nothing had ever given her the sense of power she felt at this moment. She wanted to hear Dee come.

Sliding from Dee's lap, she pulled Dee's hips to the edge of the couch and let her lips trail down and across Dee's stomach. Sandra continued her exploration until Dee was begging for release. When Sandra could no longer stand the waiting, she spread Dee's legs farther, and ran her fingers up Dee's thighs, letting her thumbs part the swollen lips until her mouth found the object of her quest.

Dee ground her hips, pushing herself into Sandra's willing mouth.

"Please, Sandra. Please, baby, now."

In response to Dee's plea, Sandra plunged her fingers deep into Dee's wet center.

"Yes," Dee cried, clamping her hands behind Sandra's head and crushing her closer.

Surprised by her need to continue touching Dee, Sandra resisted as Dee eased her up to kiss her. "Lie down," Sandra insisted. "I want more of you."

Dee gathered Sandra in her arms and pulled her down onto the couch, gazing at her. "You have beautiful eyes," she whispered, before kissing Sandra with a deep hunger.

"I want you," Sandra insisted.

"Don't worry. You'll get all of me you can handle before we're through." She placed a pillow behind Sandra's head before she turned and lay her body in the opposite direction alongside Sandra. She parted Sandra's legs and buried her face between them as she rolled onto Sandra and offered herself for Sandra's pleasure. Sandra allowed herself to sink into the incredible sensations coursing through her as Dee's mouth devoured her, while her own mouth wallowed in Dee's juices.

A long while later, Sandra lay contentedly nuzzling Dee's breasts. "Do you do everything with this kind of passion?" Dee asked.

Sandra placed her head against Dee's breast. "I've never thought of myself as a passionate person."

"You're joking." Dee looked at her, surprised.

"No. Sex never meant that much to me." She hesitated. "I've only been with one other woman. We were together for eight years, but after the first few months, she started withdrawing. She told me I was a bad lover and we stopped making love." She looked away to hide her embarrassment.

Dee took Sandra's face in her hands and looked into her eyes. "You're not a bad lover. You're one of the most passionate women I've ever been with."

"Have there been a lot of women for you?" Sandra asked out of curiosity.

It was Dee's turn to hesitate. "Yes."

She did not make any apologies. Sandra liked that.

"Does that bother you?" Dee asked.

"No. I regret not having more experiences."

"You want a little more experience tonight?" Dee asked, wiggling her eyebrows in a suggestive parody.

Sandra pushed herself against Dee. "What did you have in mind?"

"Come home with me. I'd like for you to spend the night with me."

Twenty minutes later, they were on Dee's bike headed toward her apartment. Sandra slipped her hands under Dee's jacket and manipulated her swollen nipples as the powerful bike hummed between their legs.

It took Sandra a moment to remember where she was when she woke in the strange bedroom. Dee lay on her stomach with her arms outstretched above her head. Sandra's body began to throb as she recalled the things Dee had done to her after they reached her apartment. She ran her hand across Dee's well defined back and felt her desire grow as Dee turned to her.

"Shower with me." Dee moaned as she turned over and Sandra began to kiss her breasts. "I'm going to be late for work if you keep that up."

Sandra caught a nipple between her teeth.

"Connie has a set of keys," Dee said as she rolled Sandra onto her back.

An hour later, they stood in the steamy bathroom dressing.

"Will I see you again?" Dee asked, staring at Sandra in the stream-streaked mirror.

"I'll drop in to say good-bye before I leave and I'll let you know when I get back."

"So you are coming back?"

Sandra glanced at her, surprised. "My business is here. Why wouldn't I be back? I'll only be gone for a couple of months."

Dee shrugged and grinned. "You may love the road so much you'll never want to sit behind a desk again." She ran a comb through her short wet hair.

"There's one other thing we need to discuss before we leave," Sandra said.

"What's that?" Dee asked as she turned to face her.

"Your favorite charity. We agreed you'd give me a name and I'd make a donation for whatever I thought your lessons were worth."

"Oh. Make it out to the Center for Special Children."

"I'll make it in your name. That way you'll know I made the donation."

Dee frowned. "I trust you. If you tell me you're going to do it, I know you will."

Sandra wondered how it would feel to have such complete trust in people. *I trust Dee and Laura*, she thought. *And Margaret, Ida, and Connie.* The more she thought about it the longer her list got. She smiled suddenly, grabbed Dee, and kissed her loudly on the lips. "Thank you."

Dee returned the smile and gave her a long hug.

Another hour passed before they rushed out of Dee's apartment.

CHAPTER ELEVEN

Dee and Sandra rode back to the bike shop in silence. Connie was talking to a customer when they came in. She waved to them before returning her attention to the customer.

"How do you want to handle getting your car and bike home?" Dee asked. They were standing outside her office door. Sandra was glad she was not alone with Dee. It was too hard to keep from touching her.

"Could I leave the car here until this afternoon? I'll bring someone over to drive it home," Sandra said.

"I could drive it home for you tonight," Dee offered, looking at her searchingly.

"Yes, you could, but I could also start missing you too much."

"Would that be so bad?"

"I've found my lover in bed with someone else once. I don't want that to ever happen to me again."

Dee nodded. "It probably would with me," she admitted. "I'm not ready to settle down, I guess."

"I'll never forget you."

"You make it sound like good-bye."

"Only to what happened between us last night," Sandra assured her.

"There's nothing that says we can't get together for a little fun once in awhile," Dee said.

Sandra smiled and hugged her tightly before going to retrieve her bike from the garage. Last night had been wonderful, but she could not handle a prolonged affair without a commitment.

Sandra went home and ate a breakfast hearty enough to make Margaret beam. Afterwards, she set about getting everything ready for her departure.

She called Allison, who would be handling both her personal and business affairs while she was gone.

At first, Allison had been uneasy about Sandra going off alone on a motorcycle, but the more Sandra talked about it, the more enthused Allison became.

"I think I'm jealous," she said, after listening to Sandra describe the sensation of riding.

"I could take you for a ride," Sandra said.

"No thanks," Allison replied, waving off her offer. "I'm more jealous of your two months of freedom than I am of the mode of transportation."

"Chicken."

"Absolutely!"

After hanging up, Sandra dropped a check and a letter in the mail to the Center for Special Children for fifty thousand dollars. She changed into clean jeans and a shirt before emptying her purse on to the bed. She pulled out the things she absolutely needed and found they fit quite comfortably in her

pockets. The rest she threw in a drawer. Exhaustion overtook her and she stretched out across the bed, thinking of the previous night. She drifted into a peaceful slumber with a smile on her face.

It took Sandra until the following Wednesday to get all of her affairs settled, say good-bye to the handful of friends she cared for, and to get Margaret to quit nagging her. She gave Margaret two months of paid vacation and a round trip ticket to Dublin, where Margaret's sister lived. After that, Margaret forgave her enough to allow Sandra to close up the penthouse. Margaret would stay with Minnie until she left for Ireland.

Sandra packed a small backpack. At the last moment, she took the photo of her and Mr. Peepers and slid it into her wallet. She walked away from the penthouse without looking back.

Sandra rode her bike to Laura's, where she planned to spend the night. Tomorrow morning she would begin her journey.

Sandra and Laura sat in the swing on Laura's front porch.

"You're sure you don't mind taking care of the Jag for me while I'm gone?" Sandra knew Laura was in love with the car.

Laura placed her wrist dramatically against her forehead. "It's a nasty chore, but I'll try to get through it. After all, I'd do anything for a friend."

Sandra chuckled. They swung in silence, listening to the night creatures.

"Are you going to try to find your mom?" Laura asked.

"Yes. I need to know why she left. I want to know why Dad worked so hard to keep us apart." She took a deep breath. "When I was growing up, my dad was my entire world. We

moved around so often I never really made friends. Thinking back, I see things in a different light now. The way he always insisted on being paid in cash." One of the horses, in the corral behind the cottage, blew loudly and stomped.

Sandra continued. "When I went through Dad's things after he died I never found a single canceled check, no tax returns, credit card slips. I never even found a driver's license. Don't you think that's odd?"

Laura nodded. "Did he ever give you any indication of why you moved so often?

"He always said we were moving because there was a greater chance of him getting a better paying job."

"Did you believe him?"

Sandra shrugged. "He was my father. I never thought to doubt him. Until recently, anyway."

"How do you feel about him now?"

Sandra had been asking herself the same question since reading her mother's letter. "I'm not sure. I want to believe he didn't keep us apart out of petty jealousy. I never saw him as the egotistical macho type. But maybe I never really knew him." She sighed and shook her head. "He was my dad. I don't think I could stop loving him. I just need to try and locate my mother and find out what happened."

"How will you find her?"

"I'm going to the address on the letter and see where it leads me."

"Will you spend the entire two months in San Antonio?"

Sandra shrugged. "I don't know. I'm not making any long-term plans. I'm going to take each day as it comes."

"There's hope for you yet, Tater," Laura said, squeezing Sandra's arm.

Sandra gazed into the star-riddled sky. What would tomorrow bring? She experienced a twinge of fear mixed with excitement, but she had never felt more alive.

* * * * *

The day dawned in glorious hues of pink and purple. Laura insisted Sandra eat breakfast before she left. Sandra was so anxious to get on the road she could hardly sit still. When at last she felt she could politely leave, she found herself growing hesitant.

Laura seemed to sense her sudden doubts.

"Don't get weird, Tater. This is going to be the greatest adventure of your life. This will be an adventure you can tell your grandkids about."

"I won't have grandkids," Sandra reminded her.

"Okay, so tell my grandkids." Laura hugged her tightly. "Get going before I start crying."

Unable to speak around the knot in her throat, Sandra nodded and pulled on her helmet.

All doubts left her when the bike roared to life. She smiled as adrenaline shot through her.

"Don't forget to call me," Laura yelled over the noise of the bike.

Sandra gave her a thumbs-up and slowly edged the bike toward the roadway.

City traffic made her nervous. Luckily, there was only a short stretch of heavy traffic before she reached the open roadway. Wanting to enjoy the ride and the scenery, she chose a less traveled route to San Antonio.

The wildflowers were beginning to pop up along the roadside. Sandra stopped several times to enjoy their beauty. For the first time in her life, she felt completely free. She could continue on to San Antonio to try to find her mother, or she could turn at any intersection and go wherever she pleased. The traffic was light and the sun was warm on her back. For the moment, life was almost perfect. Her only regret was no one was with her to share the beauty and excitement of the trip.

* * * * *

It was mid-afternoon before Sandra reached San Antonio. She studied a city map and memorized the directions to the address on her mother's letter. She tried not to let her hopes escalate out of control as she cruised through the quiet neighborhood. She found the address without any trouble and breathed a sigh of relief at finding the house still there.

The house was a large, two-story red-brick. Over the years, the building had been divided into apartments. She circled the block three times before she got the courage to stop. She walked up the sidewalk slowly, wondering what she would say if she were to actually find her mother. She rang the doorbell on the door marked office. When no one answered, she turned to leave with a mixture of relief and disappointment.

"Who you looking for?" a voice called.

Sandra turned, but could not see anyone. She was about to decide she had imagined it when the voice spoke again.

"I'm over here on the other side of the hedge."

Sandra walked toward the voice. "You'll have to go out to the sidewalk and come in through my gate."

Sandra followed her instructions. High hedges surrounded the house next door. She pushed the gate open, finding an older woman in a wheelchair.

"They're all out. Which one do you want?" She tugged at a wisp of curly, gray hair

"I'm trying to locate Jessica Tate. I don't know for sure if she still lives there. She lived here about thirty years ago."

"Thirty years ago!" The woman sputtered, shaking her head and making a rude noise deep in her throat. "You'd be lucky to find anyone who's been in there for thirty days." She leaned closer to Sandra. "I think they run drugs."

Shocked, Sandra looked toward the apartments. The hedges hid most of the building.

"Why are you hunting this woman? You a cop?" The woman glared at her through narrowed eyes.

"No, ma'am."

"Don't be calling me ma'am. Never liked to say it and sure

don't want to be called it. Name's Hilda Cunningham." She fixed Sandra with a sharp glare. "Who'd you say you were?"

"My name is Sandra. Mrs. Tate was a friend of my mother's and I told her I'd drop by to see if she still lived here." Sandra did not want to have to explain she was searching for her mother. She hoped the woman would not press her further for her name.

The old woman cocked her head to the side and closed one eye. "Tate, Tate. I don't remember anyone named Tate. Course I've been living here since thirty-four, so I've seen too many people come and go to remember them all, I suspect." She shook her head and stared at the apartments. "What did she look like?"

Sandra felt a sharp stab of pain. "I don't know," she replied honestly. She had no memory of her mother's face.

"Well, it doesn't matter anyway. You ain't likely to find her after all these years."

On that less-than-promising note, Sandra went to find a place to eat. She stopped at a small restaurant a few blocks away. She knew her next step should be to hire a private investigator, someone with the skills and contacts to pursue the search. Now that she was here, she was again having doubts. As she ate, she weighed the pros and cons of continuing her search. A part of her wanted to meet her mother, yet she still harbored a deep fear her mother would not want to see her and would send her away. At this point in time, she could still tell herself her mother had always loved her and there was a valid reason for her leaving. The letter helped reinforce her fantasy, but if her mother told her to leave, the rejection would be final.

When the waitress came to clear the table Sandra asked for a phone book. There were six Tates listed. None with the first name Jessica or the initial J. Opening the Yellow Pages, she copied the names and addresses of a few private investigators onto a notepad from her pocket. She might decide to call them later.

She did not know San Antonio very well. She had been here several times for conferences or an occasional meeting, but during those trips she usually only saw the route from the airport to the hotel.

San Antonio was the only major city in Texas she and her father had not lived in. She realized her dad had not taken any chances of running into her mother. She flipped through the Yellow Pages idly. Seeing a listing for restaurants, she scanned the list. During the next two months, she would probably get to know several of them quite well. Suddenly her finger froze over a listing for Peepers Diner. She saw a mental image of the photo in her wallet and the bear she held, Mr. Peepers. She started to close the book, but stopped and copied the address of the diner. *It's just a coincidence*, she told herself, but she had plenty of time for wild goose chases. Why not check it out? She paid her bill and left the restaurant. Sitting on her bike, she studied the city map. Peepers was located on the far south side of town.

Between missing her exit and getting lost while trying to double back, it took her an hour to get across town and finally find the address. She spotted the huge blue and white sign announcing Peepers while waiting at a red light.

The diner was on a small side street in the next block. The large blue and white building sat on an ample parking lot and sported a 1950s motif. *Cute idea, but a bad location*, Sandra thought.

The light changed and she started forward. She was studying the building when a car darted out from behind a long row of high oleander bushes.

Instinct guided her. She knew she was going to hit the car. She turned her bike into a slide and managed to roll free as Dee had taught her, just before her bike slammed into the car. Stunned, she lay against the curb. Her left shoulder throbbed. She slowly took assessment of the rest of her body. Nothing seemed to be broken. Sandra heard the rustle of clothing as someone knelt beside her. She rolled over onto her back.

"Don't move him," a voice commanded.

"He's moving himself," a second voice answered.

Sandra's shock was wearing off. She flipped up the visor on her helmet and started to sit up.

"I don't think you should move."

She looked up to see a woman with emerald green eyes filled with concern. An extremely short blond buzz-cut and a strong, slightly squared chin projected a sense of strength and determination.

These eyes are real, no contact enhancement here, Sandra thought.

The woman's arm went around Sandra's shoulder and supported her. Sandra's heart did a rare tat-a-tat.

"Why don't you lie back," the woman instructed as she cradled Sandra's head on her lap.

Maybe I shouldn't get up too quickly, Sandra reasoned as she continued to stare into the woman's mesmerizing eyes.

"Someone has gone to call an ambulance. It'll be here soon," the woman assured her.

That bit of news shook Sandra from her mooning.

"I'm fine," she replied, regretfully pulling away from the woman and inching her way to her feet.

The woman kept a firm grip on her arm.

"I'm fine, really," Sandra assured her as she removed her helmet. She heard the woman's breath catch when Sandra turned to face her. For a long second, their gazes held.

The arrival of a police car shattered the moment. Glancing around, Sandra was surprised to find a small crowd gathered around them. She located her bike. The front tire was under the car. She felt a wave of pain and anger. Dee had warned her about people who never paid attention to motorcycles. She glared at the crowd around her.

"Who hit me?" she demanded as she turned back to the woman. She would prosecute the careless fool who had destroyed her beautiful bike.

"I did," the woman replied.

Before Sandra could retort, two police officers approached them. One of the officers led Sandra off to interview her.

He was a middle-aged man with a face so deeply lined Sandra wondered what he had witnessed during his life to age him so.

"I'm Patrolman Peterson. Are you hurt?" he asked.

Sandra rotated her shoulder. "I banged my shoulder, but nothing is broken."

He nodded. "All right. Tell me what happened," he said as he removed a pen from his pocket.

"I had just pulled away from the light," Sandra said, pointing at the traffic light behind him. "The next thing I know a car came flying out in front of me."

He studied the traffic light, the driveway from which the car came, and the accident site itself.

"You're lucky the bike slid," Peterson said as he eyed the bike beneath the car.

"I had a good teacher," she replied as she looked at her bike. Dee's guilt and persistence had probably saved her life, or at the very least, prevented her from sustaining serious injury.

The patrolman began to write out the accident report, and Sandra turned her attention back to him. He asked her a few more questions about the accident. After discovering she was passing through San Antonio, he took down her Dallas address and recommended several downtown hotels she could stay in until the repairs on her bike were completed. As he was reciting the list of hotels, an ambulance arrived.

"Since they are already here, you ought to let them take you in and have your shoulder x-rayed," he said.

Sandra declined. She did not need a doctor. Her suit and the helmet had protected her from the pavement. Her shoulder throbbed. She was sure a nasty bruise would result by morning. Checking her shoulder movement carefully, she was certain no permanent damage existed.

The woman who hit her bike was shouting at the other police officer.

"Guess I'd better go see what's happening over there," Peterson said. "If we need anything else from you, Ms. Tate, we'll contact you."

Sandra thanked him and followed him to see why the woman was shouting.

"I've called the city about those oleanders a dozen times," she insisted. "I've told them someone was going to get hurt." Peterson began talking to her, and the woman's voice lowered.

Sandra looked at the bushes. They really were a hazard. She walked into the driveway and stood where a car would normally set before pulling out. She was not able to see the street. She kept moving forward until she could see around the oleanders. A car would have to be in the street before the driver could see clearly.

An EMS technician approached Sandra. "Are you hurt? You seem to be moving around pretty good."

"I hit my shoulder, but it's okay."

"Let me take a look at it just to be safe?"

Sandra started to argue but realized it would be faster and less hassle to go ahead and let him. It would also help her case when she told Laura and Allison. An accident on her first day was not going to look too good. She did not want to think about the lecture she would get from Margaret, if she heard about the accident. Sandra certainly did not intend to tell her.

"You're lucky you were wearing a jacket. The pavement would have messed you up bad," the tech said, probing Sandra's shoulder. "It's already bruising. You should see a doctor."

"I'll go in later if it keeps bothering me," Sandra promised. She was again watching the woman who hit her bike. She had finished talking to the police officers and was standing by her car staring at Sandra's bike. Sandra thanked the tech and walked to her bike.

"I'm really sorry," the woman said, as Sandra draped her jacket across her arm.

"You came out of the driveway like a bat out of hell," Sandra accused, trying to keep her anger in check. She knew the oleanders blocked the woman's view, but they had not grown there overnight. The bushes had obviously been a safety issue for some time.

The woman looked at her. "I didn't see you coming until it was too late. I was trying to get out of your way."

Sandra felt sick looking at the mangled wheel of her beautiful bike. She shuddered when she realized what could have happened to her without Dee's coaching.

"Are you all right?"

Sandra pulled on her ripped jacket despite the warmth of the day.

"Where do you want the bike to go?"

Sandra turned to find a tall, thin guy with a clipboard in hand. He was wearing a drab green shirt with a tag that read Feltz Towing Service. She hesitated, uncertain where she should send her bike for repairs.

"I know a guy who has a shop near here. He's really good with bikes," the woman offered.

"Do you work on a commission? A percentage of everything you can run over and send him?" Sandra snapped, instantly regretting her childish outburst.

The woman's voice filled with exasperation and her gaze locked onto Sandra. "I'm trying to help. I've already told you I'm sorry about this," she said, waving her hand at the wreckage.

"Being sorry won't fix my bike," Sandra argued. She turned to the tow truck driver. "Is there a Honda dealership in town?"

The guy removed a battered Spurs basketball cap and scratched his balding head. "I don't know much about motorcycles. I can call the dispatcher and have her check around."

Sandra sensed a major hassle about to start and did not

want to spend the next hour dealing with it. "Is your friend really any good?" she asked the woman while staring at the restaurant.

"He's the best in town," she assured her.

"What's the address?"

The woman retrieved a day planner from her car and gave the driver the address.

Sandra wrote the address and telephone number for Bill's Motorcycle Repair and Body Shop in her note pad before turning to the driver. "Tell them I'll be over to take care of the paperwork later."

He started to protest, but Sandra nailed him with her best boardroom glare. He shrugged, handed her a clipboard of papers to sign, and went to work.

Sandra cringed as he hooked the front of the car to the tow truck and raised the front end up enough to pull her bike free. The police officers and a bystander helped the driver load the bike onto the back of the truck. He lowered the car, unhooked it, and left. Other than a small dent at the bottom of the door, the car seemed no worse for wear.

To Sandra's consternation, the police officers were directing the woman to pull her car back into the parking lot. The woman would now have to pull back out into traffic. "She will probably run over someone else," she growled to no one in particular and started toward the restaurant.

"Can I drive you somewhere?" the woman called after her.

"I was headed to the restaurant to talk to the owner," she said without slowing.

"What for?"

Sandra stopped and turned back to the woman, astounded at her boldness.

"I'm sorry," the woman stuttered, sensing Sandra's shock. "I'm the owner," she explained, turning off the ignition and getting out of her car. "I'm Cory Gallager," she said, extending her hand.

Sandra could not help but notice the woman's long thin

fingers, even as the words and their meaning sank in. A part of her had been hoping her mother was the owner of the diner.

"I'm Sandra," she said and tried to hide her disappointment.

"What did you need to see me about?" Cory asked.

Sandra hesitated. It suddenly seemed ridiculous to say, *I was just stopping by to ask how your restaurant got its name.* It no longer mattered. This woman could not possibly be her mother.

Sandra stared at the diner's sign. She had a gut feeling there were answers here, and her instincts were seldom wrong. She looked back at the woman's green eyes. Could she be the attraction drawing her to this place?

"Are you from the employment agency about the dish washing job?" Cory inquired, slowly taking in Sandra's clothes.

Sandra almost laughed.

"It's only part-time. I have an employee out on disability," Cory continued. "So the job's only good for about six weeks."

"That's perfect." Sandra looked around to see if she had actually spoken the words or someone else had. She experienced a brief moment of doubt about her decision. Was it curiosity about the restaurant, or about its owner?

Cory was still watching her. "You know the job only pays minimum wage, and you'll be working a split shift."

Sandra did some quick calculation and tried not to smile. Her firm spent more on pencils each month. "That's fine," she said.

Cory seemed to hesitate. "Do you have any experience or references?"

"To wash dishes?" Sandra asked dumbfounded. "How much experience do I need?"

A mischievous grin crept across Cory's face. "Be here at ten tomorrow morning. We don't serve breakfast, but we have a heavy lunch crowd."

"I'll be here," Sandra assured her. She contemplated what

to do next. She had no idea how far away Bill's Motorcycle Repair and Body Shop was. The odds were against it being within walking distance. She cursed her decision not to ride along in the tow truck.

"Let me drive you to Bill's."

Sandra started to protest, but looked into Cory's green eyes and relented.

"Do you live around here?" Cory asked as they pulled out into traffic.

"No," Sandra replied without thinking.

"Where do you live?"

Sandra gave her the only address in town she knew, the apartment where her mother had once lived.

Cory chewed her lip. "I don't mean to be nosy, but how are you going to get to work? That's all the way across town."

Sandra squirmed. "I have insurance on the bike. I'll have a rental car until it's repaired."

Cory nodded, but a frown still creased her forehead. They remained silent until they pulled into Bill's small parking lot a few minutes later.

"Sandra," Cory started and stopped. She seemed to be trying to say something, but shook her head instead. She reached into the car's ashtray and removed a business card. "Here's the number to the restaurant." She pulled a pen from over the visor and scribbled on the back of the card. "That's my home number. Call me if something happens or you run into any hassles with getting the car and can't make it in tomorrow." She hesitated. "Sandra, I'm really sorry about hitting your bike. I'm so grateful you weren't injured."

"Thanks." Sandra took the card and got out. "I'll see you tomorrow morning." Again for a brief moment their gaze held, and Sandra felt a warm shiver race over her.

CHAPTER TWELVE

After dealing with the mechanic, the insurance company, and arranging for a rental car, Sandra found a nice motel located near the diner. The check-in clerk almost dropped her teeth when Sandra told her she wanted the room for six weeks. If the search at the diner failed to pan out, she could always leave sooner. After settling in her room, she called Laura. It took Sandra a few minutes to convince Laura she was uninjured, but eventually, they were able to laugh together about Sandra's first day of rambling and her great new job.

Later, Sandra called Allison and started the process to avenge the mangling of her bike. She knew enough of the right people in San Antonio to get some action started.

At six she drove to Peepers for dinner and to survey her revenge. She smiled brightly at the city crewmen who were busy cutting down the long row of oleanders.

Stepping inside the diner was like taking a step back into the 1950s.

"Booth or counter," the hostess asked.

"Booth," Sandra said, as Buddy Holly began to sing his love of Peggy Sue. The hostess was a bubbly young woman who chattered non-stop as she escorted Sandra to a booth near the back. She sat a glass of water and silverware down and turned to leave.

"How did the diner get its name?" Sandra asked, trying not to let the anxiousness show in her voice.

The woman stopped and seemed to consider the question for a moment. "You know, I don't know. I don't think anyone has ever asked me that question before. I could ask the owner," she offered cheerfully.

"No!" Sandra replied quickly. "It's not important. I was just curious."

After assuring Sandra someone would be right with her to take her order, the young woman rushed off to seat the next group of guests.

When the waitress arrived to take her food order, Sandra realized she was starving. Despite its fifties motif, the diner didn't specialize in just burgers. There was a nice selection of entrées. Sandra was further surprised by its great wine selection. She ordered the baked chicken with wild rice and a glass of chardonnay.

Sandra studied the activity around her as she sipped her wine and waited for her food. The diner was busy. She had obviously been mistaken about its location hurting business. Enjoying the music, she leaned back and took in the polished black-and-white-checkered tile and chrome gleaming throughout the diner. A large glass display case sat against the far wall. Inside it, Sandra could see several trophies, a poodle skirt, a pair of saddle oxfords, and a large photo of Elvis.

A long counter ran across the front of the diner. Several people sat on the red vinyl and chrome stools lining the counter. Sandra wished she had checked the menu to see if the diner served ice cream sodas. This was the kind of place her father would have enjoyed. Occasionally, there would be a few extra dollars and he would take them out to eat as a special treat.

The arrival of her food brought her perusal of the diner's décor to a halt. Sandra ate slowly, savoring every bite. Laura would be pleased to learn she was taking the time to enjoy her food. The chicken and wine were excellent. Sandra could not remember getting better food at any of Dallas' finer restaurants.

She paid the tab, adding a generous tip for the wonderful service. She was standing to leave when she bumped into someone. She turned to apologize and found herself staring into those emerald green eyes again.

"It's either fate or we're both accident-prone," Sandra said, unable to look away.

Cory's gaze broke away and settled on the large tip still lying on the table. Sandra saw the frown reappear. *Now she's wondering how a previously unemployed dishwasher can afford to leave that kind of tip*, Sandra groaned to herself.

"I don't believe in fate," Cory stated, and eyed Sandra's tailored slacks and jacket. An awkward silence fell between them.

"I'll see you tomorrow," Sandra said, before making a hasty exit.

Dressed in sharply creased black slacks and a white silk shirt, Sandra arrived at the diner ten minutes early. Cory sat at a table with four other women. She looked up as Sandra entered, and again, did a visual survey of her clothes before motioning for her to join them. Cory stood as Sandra approached.

"Everyone, this is Sandra." She stopped. "I'm sorry, I don't remember your last name."

Sandra hesitated. Would anyone recognize her name? *Stop being stupid*, she admonished herself. *It's not as though you're a household name.* "Tate," she answered.

"Tate?" A small frown creased Cory's forehead.

Sandra held her breath, as Cory studied her face.

After a moment Cory shook her head slightly and turned to the group.

"Sandra will be taking Pat's place while she's out. Sandra, this is Louise, our hostess."

Sandra shook hands with the bubbly young woman she had met the night before.

"Anna and Ginny are two of our waitresses. You'll meet the other two tonight," Cory said.

Dyke, Sandra thought as she shook hands with Anna, a short woman with curly brown hair and a permanent pout.

Ginny was a tall, lanky brunette. She wore over-sized, tortoise shell glasses that gave her a wise, bookish appearance.

"Glad to have you aboard," Ginny said as she gave Sandra's hand a limp shake.

"Ginny is ex-Navy," Anna explained. "She has her own vocabulary."

Everyone laughed.

Cory turned to the other woman at the booth. "This is Maria, one of our cooks."

Sandra guessed Maria to be in her fifties. She combed her short salt-and-pepper hair to one side in much the same way as Sandra's father had worn his.

"Nice to meet you, Sandra," Maria said in a voice sweetened by the faintest of accents.

It hit Sandra suddenly. *All these women are gay.* Cory had definitely made Peepers a family place.

The front door opened and a man walked in.

"And that," Ginny grimaced, "is a customer."

"Time to go to work," Cory said with a wide smile that made Sandra's breath catch. Cory picked up a coffee cup from the table. "Come on, Sandra. I'll show you where everything is." Her eyes again ran over Sandra's clothing. "I should have warned you to wear something more casual."

Sandra looked down at her clothes. She thought she was pretty casual. After all, everybody else was wearing nice slacks and blouses.

"This way," Cory directed, leading Sandra into the kitchen. "Our system is an older one, but it still works, so I can't justify replacing it. Basically, what you do is dump the leftovers in this barrel, spray the excess off here, and stack the dishes in these racks." She moved along a gleaming metal table with an odd circular depression in the center that looked similar to a sink. "When you fill a rack, slide it into this opening. The clean dishes come out over here and then you stack them over there on those shelves for Maria and Wilma, the other cook." She turned to look at Sandra. "Any questions?"

Sandra shook her head and smiled smugly. She had managed a major architectural firm for years. Washing a few dishes would not over-tax her brain cells. "I think I can handle it," she replied.

Cory did not look convinced. "Here's an apron." She pulled a large plastic apron from a hook and handed it to her. "You'll have to be fast. The lunch crowd is heavy."

A heavy-set, African-American woman came through an outside door on the far side of the kitchen. "That's Wilma, our second cook," Cory explained. "After everything calms down I'll introduce you to her and the other waitresses. I have to get back out front, but I'll try to check on you from time to time. Just tell one of the waitresses if you need anything. They'll know where to find me."

For the first time Sandra felt a twinge of panic. *Two cooks. How many more waitresses? How busy would the place get?*

Cory stood by as Sandra pulled on the apron. It was so large it wrapped completely around her. She tied it tightly. Cory was still eyeing Sandra's clothes. "I think I have an old T-shirt in my car that will fit you. I'll go get it and you can change? You're going to ruin your shirt."

Sandra felt a stab of annoyance. She had walked through construction sites and city sewers in a suit and heels. She could certainly survive washing a few dishes. Besides, the mammoth apron encased her. There was no way anything could get to her. "No, thanks. I'll be fine."

Forty minutes later, piles of dirty dishes surrounded Sandra, and she was completely drenched. In fact, everything within ten feet of her was drenched. No matter how many dishes she washed, a hundred more sprang up to take their place. The work area surrounding her became a jungle of steam, water, and dirty dishes. Anna, one of the waitresses, came in, took one look at Sandra and burst out laughing. Hurrying out of the kitchen with fresh pitchers of tea, Anna called over her shoulder to Sandra. "Better get a move on. The rush hasn't even hit yet."

Seconds later, Cory rushed in looking rather harried. "Anna said you were having problems. Do you want me to come back and help you?"

Sandra was mortified. "No, I'm fine."

Cory looked at the pile of dirty dishes. "Then get moving. You're way behind," she said and left.

Sandra considered ripping off the apron and stuffing it down Cory's throat, but pride forced her to finish what she started. She took a deep breath and looked at the mess around her. This was ridiculous. It was time to take control of this chaos. All she needed was a system. It was a simple matter of organization and project management. She moved the rack for the rinsed dishes to her left, pushed the dirty dishes into a pile closer to her and shoved the scrap barrel until it was at her right side. It took several minutes for her body to learn the new movements of the job, but slowly the repetition grew into a rhythm and she began to catch up. By the time Ginny came in with what she promised was the last of the dirty dishes, Sandra was only four trays behind.

Cory came in as Sandra was pulling the last tray out of the sterilizer. She stopped, open mouthed, and stared. "I'm impressed," she said, nodding her approval. "I was afraid I'd have to rent a back hoe to dig you out by now." Her smile sent a ray of sunshine into Sandra's heart.

Inordinately pleased by Cory's praise, Sandra could not keep from smiling as she pulled the apron off.

"I've never been so physically tired in my life," Sandra admitted as she turned from hanging up the apron.

Cory groaned.

Sandra followed her gaze and was shocked to see she was soaking wet. The sleeves of her shirt that she had rolled above her elbows were a kaleidoscope of colors ranging from ketchup to broccoli.

"Don't suppose I get paid for wearing the menu, huh?" Sandra joked.

Cory flashed a lazy smile. Her deep throaty laugh caused Sandra to forget all about the struggle of the past two and a half hours.

When Sandra returned at four to start the second half of her shift, she was dressed in a Spurs T-shirt and faded jeans. A shopping trip to a discount-clothing store netted her a new work wardrobe of jeans and T-shirts. She treated herself by purchasing a new pair of sneakers with thick rubber soles.

Cory nodded and smiled when she saw Sandra going into the kitchen. Sandra felt the unfamiliar flame shoot through her again. The remainder of the shift was much easier, thanks in part to her new routine and in part to the warm memory of Cory's smile.

After the dinner crowd left, the entire staff sat around and chatted while the waitresses counted their tips. Sandra was so exhausted she felt numb. Cory appeared with a tray of beers.

"Sandra, do you want a glass?" she asked, setting the tray down on the table.

"Not if it has to be washed," Sandra managed.

Everyone but Anna, who kept staring at Sandra, laughed and took a beer.

Cory settled into the chair beside Sandra. Her leg brushed lightly against Sandra's, causing an electrical jolt to shoot through Sandra's body.

Sandra tried to keep up with the idle chatter, but between her exhaustion and the havoc Cory's closeness was creating, it was too much effort. She wanted nothing more than to be able to collapse into bed. She stole a glance at Cory, but refused to let her imagination slip away to where it was attempting to go. As soon as the drinks were finished, everyone but Cory and Anna rose to leave. Grateful, she was free to escape, Sandra stood.

"Oh, Sandra," Cory said. "I almost forgot. I need you to fill out some paperwork. I should have had you do it yesterday. It won't take but a minute. Would you mind doing it now?"

"No. That's fine." Sandra tried to hide her disappointment as she slid back into her seat. Cory left to go to her office in the back.

"How badly was your bike damaged?" Anna asked.

"I called the repair shop after lunch. The front wheel needs to be replaced and there's some mechanical repair work. Bill, the owner, thinks he can have it fixed by the end of next week, if he can find all the parts."

"Nice bike. I saw it when they were loading it up." Anna leaned back and spread her arms across the top of the booth. Her shirt pulled tight across her breasts, but Sandra was too tired to appreciate the view.

"Thanks."

"After you get it fixed maybe you could take me for a ride sometime. Or even before you get the bike back, if you'd like."

Shocked by the obvious come-on, Sandra looked up. Anna smiled and winked. Sandra was saved from a response by Cory's return.

"I'll wait for you in the car," Anna told Cory and headed out.

"Okay, babe. I'll be there in a minute."

Cory and Anna together. Sandra experienced a sharp pang of disappointment. She felt an almost uncontrollable urge to tell Cory about Anna's flirting. *That would be real smart*, she admonished herself.

Sandra sat staring at the forms. She would have to lie about her references and education. Oh well, the worse that could happen was she would get fired. She picked up the pen and began filling out the form. She made up her work references from restaurants in Dallas, hoping Cory would not check them.

"The law requires me to ask for two forms of ID," Cory said.

Sandra's heart flew to her throat. Lying was hard. What if Cory knew Dallas well enough to recognize the address on her license was in a highly exclusive part of the city? How was she going to explain living there? Cory would certainly fire her. A part of Sandra enjoyed being an unknown dishwasher. She was not ready to give up her anonymity yet. *Lie and stall*, she decided.

"My wallet is in the car. I'm used to having everything with me on my bike. I can't seem to get organized with a car." She was ashamed of her low-handed attempt to make Cory feel so bad she'd forget about the ID. Seeing the flicker of guilt wash over Cory's face, made her even more ashamed.

"Bring them in tomorrow," Cory offered.

Sandra concentrated her attention on the form to hide her

embarrassment. There was a blank for drivers license number and she filled it in with her actual number.

"Have you heard how badly your bike was damaged?" Cory asked. "I can't tell you how sorry I am about all of that."

She did indeed sound sorry. While she finished filling out the forms, Sandra repeated what Bill had told her.

"At least the city finally got off its duff and cut those damn oleanders down. I've been after them for ages," Cory stated as she took the forms from Sandra and studied them. "Tate," she said with a frown and glanced again at Sandra before slightly shaking her head.

"Something wrong?" Sandra asked, her heart pounding. *I don't lie well*, she decided.

"No. Everything seems to be fine. I just have this feeling, I should know you." She looked at Sandra and shook her head. "The job is only for six weeks," she added softly.

Sandra wondered if the reminder was meant for her or for Cory herself.

CHAPTER THIRTEEN

Time was slipping away. Sandra had been in San Antonio for three weeks. After work, she was usually so tired she went straight to the motel and slept. She struggled to keep her feelings for Cory under control. Her free time was spent trying to locate her mother. The telephone number mentioned by her mother in the letter was miraculously still valid, but no one currently there could remember Jessica Tate, and the employment records for that time-period had long since been archived. The secretary Sandra spoke with was sympathetic, but reminded Sandra that even if they did have the records, she could not release any personal information from them.

Sandra spent hours at the library combing through city directories, and discovered a J Tate listed as living on Westhaven. After checking the Westhaven address and finding a parking lot, she realized she had reached the limit of her detective skills. She made up her mind to hire a private investigator, as soon as she returned to Dallas.

Sandra hung up her apron and grabbed her helmet. It was Sunday night and she was off the following two days. She had picked up her bike the day before. The repairs had taken much longer than anticipated, due to a problem in locating a replacement part. Cory was right about Bill; the bike looked brand new.

Sandra was looking forward to riding her bike to the coast. She was ready for some sun and lazy hours. The dinner rush had been heavy tonight, and it had taken her longer than usual to finish. On her way out, Sandra found Cory sitting alone at a table totally absorbed in something in front of her. As Sandra grew nearer, she saw it was a set of blueprints and felt a familiar rush of adrenaline.

"Are you building a house, or adding on to the diner?"

Cory let the plans roll shut and looked around embarrassed. "Uh, no," she stammered.

Sandra felt good about her upcoming time off and could not resist teasing Cory. "Come on. What were you so engrossed in?"

"It's nothing really. A stupid pipe dream." Cory picked up the blueprints and placed them on a folder at the edge of the table.

Sandra stopped teasing. "There's nothing stupid about dreams. Where would the world be without dreamers?"

Cory looked at her for a long second before shrugging and glancing back at the rolled up blueprints.

"It's a house I wanted to buy and renovate. When I was a kid my parents used to drive by the house when they took us to the coast. Every time we drove by it, Dad would tell us about the dream he and Mom had of buying the house. Of course, he could never have afforded it on his pay. He worked at one of the Air Force bases and it took everything he made to feed and clothe us. There were five of us kids," Cory explained.

Not wanting to do anything that would stop Cory from talking, Sandra nodded.

"Anyway, we would spend the travel time to the coast planning the changes we would make to the house and yard." She laughed. "The only change my mom ever wanted was to plant an apple tree in the front yard." She stopped and shrugged. "Both of my parents are dead, but their dream became mine."

"It sounds like a wonderful dream," Sandra said. "Can I see the blueprints?"

Hesitantly, Cory opened the prints and used the salt and pepper shakers to help hold them open. As Cory moved the folder out of the way, a photo fell. Sandra leaned over and picked it up.

"That's the shape it's in now," Cory explained, almost apologetically. "The foundation is sound. It just needs some TLC."

"Wow! It's a nineteenth century Italianate Victorian!" Sandra exclaimed in awe of the graceful, if somewhat deteriorating, structure.

"How did you know that?" Cory asked, amazed.

"Architecture's a hobby of mine."

Cory nodded. "I fell in love with this place the first time I saw it. A cattle baron built the house in 1853. It's located south of town about twenty miles out and surrounded by thirty acres of some of the most beautiful landscaping you've ever seen. Of course, it needs a lot of work too."

"Who owns it?"

"Alexander Hall, a banker, owned it for years. He died about six years ago and left it to his son. The son kept hanging onto the place, but didn't maintain it, as you can see. It went on the market about two weeks ago."

"Have you put a bid in?"

Cory shook her head. "No. I can't afford to buy the place. Like I said, it's a pipe dream."

Seeing the pain in Cory's eyes, Sandra felt a strong wave of protectiveness toward her. Pushing it away, she studied the blueprints.

"Are these the changes you want?"

"Yeah. I wanted to restore it to its original condition."

Sandra became lost in the world she loved. "You've done a good job of maintaining the integrity, but if you want to hold it true to the original specifications, you need to remove these bay windows. They wouldn't have been in the original design." She grabbed a pencil and began to lightly sketch her suggestions onto the back of the folder. By the time she was through, she had a line drawing of the front of the house and Cory was again staring at her.

"Who are you?" Cory asked.

Sandra laid the pencil down, knowing she'd gotten too carried away. "What difference does it make?"

"You're not who you're pretending to be. That generally means you have something to hide."

"Everyone has something to hide."

"Are you running from the law?"

"No, and it's a good thing I wasn't or you would have gotten me bagged the day we met," Sandra said, trying to make it sound like a joke, but instead Cory grimaced.

"Then why are you washing dishes for minimum wage? It's pretty obvious you have money."

"What's so obvious? I could be in hock up to my ears."

Cory shook her head. "You didn't flinch when you ruined a hundred dollar silk shirt. My guess is, your bike cost more than my car. You haven't cashed any of your weekly pay checks. And you've never shown me your ID."

Sandra sighed and played with the corner of the folder. "I'm not a danger to anyone, and I'll be gone in three weeks. Can't we just let it go at that?"

"Is Sandra Tate your real name?"

Sandra hesitated before replying, "Yes."

Cory watched her. "You're still lying to me about something. You know it's illegal to falsify employment records."

"You have my word. I'm Sandra Tate, and I'm not here to hurt anyone."

Cory frowned. "Sandra, I like you. You're a great worker, but I have a responsibility to myself, the diner, and the women who work for me."

"I won't let you down," Sandra promised. For some reason, she wanted to keep this job. The honest simplicity provided something she needed. She could not explain it. She just knew she wanted things to remain the way they were for a little while longer. In three weeks she would go back to Dallas and pick up the reins to Tate Enterprises, but for now she wanted to be Sandra Tate, dishwasher.

Cory stared at her hard as if trying to read her mind. Sandra felt a warm glow start deep inside her and spread as they sat inches from each other. As if on its own volition, her hand came up and gently cupped Cory's cheek. When she did not pull away, Sandra leaned forward and kissed her gently.

"I won't let you down," she promised again. "And I won't do anything to hurt you." Shocked, she saw tears flood Cory's eyes.

"You already have," Cory whispered, grabbing the blueprints and folder. "Please, leave. I need to close up and get home." Cory stood and turned her back to Sandra.

Sandra remembered that Anna and Cory always rode together. "Are you and Anna together?"

Cory's shoulders shifted slightly and straighten. "Anna lives a block away from me. She has two kids and is barely making ends meet. She rides with me because she can't afford to drive." Cory sniffed.

"Is there someone else?"

"No."

"Then how have I hurt you?"

"There's no trust in you, yet you've taken advantage of the trust of everyone who works here."

"I never intended to hurt anyone."

"Then what did you intend to do?"

Sandra recalled Laura's advice to be more spontaneous.

"I'm looking for my mother. She left me when I was a child and I know she lived and worked in San Antonio for awhile after she left. Beyond that, I've not been able to find anything."

Cory turned back to face her. "What has that got to do with you working here?" Her breath caught. "Does your mother work here?"

Sandra shook her head. "I saw the name of the diner in the phone book. The only thing I have from my childhood is a photo of me clutching a bear. I remember his name was Mr. Peepers."

Cory sat down, picked up the salt shaker, and began turning it in circles on the table as Sandra continued.

"The shadow of the person taking the photo can be seen at the bottom of the shot. I think it's my mother."

"How old would your mother be? What does she look like?" Cory fired the questions rapidly, but kept her attention focused on the salt shaker.

"She would be in her late-fifties, early sixties," Sandra said, shocked when she realized she did not know how old her mother was. "I don't know what she looks like. If there were any photos of her, Dad must have thrown them out after the divorce. He never talked about her." Sandra thought Cory looked relieved.

"It must have been a bitter divorce."

"I don't remember any of it."

"You never asked your dad about her?"

Sandra shook her head. "No. I guess I felt too guilty. I thought it was my fault she left."

"You don't still believe that do you?"

"No. I guess not." Tears tightened Sandra's throat. She began to twist the ring on her finger.

Cory reached out and touched Sandra's hand.

The touch was soft, but galvanized Sandra to her chair. Before she could react, Cory removed her hand.

"How did you know to look for your mom in San Antonio?" Cory asked.

Sandra tried to ignore the desire Cory's touch had sparked. She concentrated on telling Cory about her father's death and about finding the letter in his wallet.

"You just found the letter, and you're now living where your mother once lived." Cory was clearly confused.

"I don't live there," Sandra admitted. "It was the only address I knew to give you."

Cory rubbed her temples. "Of course. Another lie."

"Who did you buy the diner from?" Sandra asked, avoiding Cory's biting remark.

"Nelda Rodgers. I've known Nelda for years. I worked here while I was going to college. I was in college studying to be an interior decorator, but I fell in love with the hustle and bustle of the diner. I ended up dropping out of college and managing the diner for Nelda after she retired. A couple of years after she retired she decided to move from San Antonio and put the diner up for sale. I asked her to sell it to me. She took a big chance and owner-financed. She and her partner JJ are dear friends of mine."

Cory shook her head. "I'm sorry, but I don't see how the diner could have anything to do with your mom. Nelda inherited it from her folks. They opened the diner when she was a kid. Nelda has never been married and doesn't have children."

Sandra slumped into a chair, defeated. She had been so sure the diner was a lead to her mother. The whole thing had been a long shot. Other than the name, there had been nothing to suggest any connection between her mother and the diner. She realized Cory was talking to her. "What did you say?"

"I asked what you planned to do if you found your mom?"

"Nothing. I guess I just wanted to see her."

"You mean you never intended to tell her who you are?"

Sandra shrugged. "Probably not. It's been so long. She no doubt has another family by now." Sandra stood. "I'll see you Wednesday."

"You're going to continue working?"

"Unless you've fired me."

Cory squinted at her. "But why? You said you were only working here because you thought there was some connection to your mom. Why keep working? You obviously don't need the money."

"I told you I'd work for six weeks, and I'll do it."

"I could probably find someone else, if you'd rather not."

Sandra shook her head and left. She rode in a daze, letting the wind whip around her. The disappointment in losing her best lead to her mother sat heavy on her. She tried to lighten it by recalling Cory's lips on hers, but the tears in Cory's eyes left her feeling guilty. She had made a mess of everything. Maybe it would be better for everyone if she did leave.

She rode around the city until exhaustion forced her back to the motel. As tired as she was, sleep was slow in coming. The eastern sky was growing light when she decided to cancel her trip to the coast; it no longer seemed worth the effort. After taking her clothes to a laundromat, she spent the rest of her time off, sitting in her motel room staring at the television. Not even a call from Laura could lift her out of her funk.

Cory seemed to be around a lot more during the following week. Neither of them mentioned the kiss nor their conversation. At times, Sandra wondered if she had dreamed the kiss.

Cory caught her as she was leaving after the lunch rush on Friday. "Can you come into my office for a minute, please?"

Sandra followed her without comment.

Cory closed the door behind them. "I was wondering, since you don't know anyone in San Antonio, if you'd like to come to dinner on Monday night."

Sandra could not hide her surprise. She watched in silence as Cory nervously rearranged the things on her desk.

"I have a couple of friends coming in who live in Rockport. I thought it'd be nice if you could meet other people," Cory said.

"I'll be gone in two weeks," Sandra said, to remind herself more so than Cory.

"Which is why it's safe to invite you."

Sandra continued to gaze at Cory, but Cory's eyes wouldn't meet hers. "Okay. What time?"

"Around seven."

"Can I bring anything?" Sandra asked.

When Cory hesitated, Sandra volunteered, "I could pick up the wine."

"Are you sure?"

"Yeah. What are you fixing?"

"Bring something to go with fish."

Sandra nodded and stood. "I'll see you then."

Sandra managed to control her jubilation until she reached her motel room. Turning on the television she began to dance around the room. Laughter burst forth, and she forced herself to stop with a firm reminder she would be leaving in a few days. Cory was only being nice to her.

Sandra spent Monday morning shopping for the right outfit. She needed something that did not look horribly expensive, but fit her like it was. Nothing she found was right. She finally gave up and bought a pale rose western shirt and a black leather vest. She wore them with her black jeans and boots. She went to three different liquor stores before she found the wine she wanted. She considered getting her hair cut, but at the last minute she decided not to, since the helmet would destroy anything she did.

She was ready two hours early. She paced her motel room, which grew steadily smaller with each circuit. *Why am I being such a fool? Cory doesn't care about me in any way other than friendship. She only invited me over because she felt sorry for me.*

Unable to wait any longer, Sandra climbed on her bike and made her way to the address Cory had given her. It was only a few blocks away and she arrived ten minutes early. She made several trips through the surrounding blocks to burn time.

When she finally pulled into Cory's driveway there was a black kingcab truck sitting in front of the small bungalow. Trying to tame the wild butterflies in her stomach, she rang the doorbell. Cory swept the door open, and Sandra's breath caught at the sight of her dressed in crisp white slacks and a green cotton shirt that highlighted her eyes. She saw Cory's eyes assess and approve of the clothes she was wearing. Sandra handed her the wine. Cory noted the expensive label and nodded in appreciation. She glanced back over her shoulder before stepping closer to Sandra.

"Will you do me one favor?" she asked, keeping her voice low.

"If I can." Sandra's heart missed a beat. She'd do anything for this woman.

"Before you leave to go back to wherever you're from, will you tell me who you really are?"

"I've already told you."

"No. I mean who are you, really?"

"I'm Sandra Tate. I'm an architect from Dallas. I came to San Antonio to locate my mother and to rest."

"Jesus Christ." Cory paled and swayed. Sandra held out a

hand to steady her. "That's why your name kept sounding so familiar. I just read an article on you in *Texas Business Review*."

Before Sandra could respond, a voice called out. "Cory, is everything all right?" An older woman, slightly shorter than Sandra came into view. Her long, salt and pepper hair was caught in a large silver clasp. She looked regal in a long loose-flowing skirt with a bright multi-colored blouse. She flashed a warm contagious smile. "Hello, there."

Startled, Cory stepped back to let Sandra in. " Nelda, this is Sandra." Cory's eyes met Sandra's. "Nelda used to own Peepers."

Sandra stared hard at the woman as Cory closed the door behind her. *What am I looking for?* she wondered.

"How did the diner come by its name?" Sandra almost choked on the words as she shook Nelda's hand.

"My dad named it after a silly old song." Nelda enthusiastically sang a line, but Sandra wasn't paying attention. The diner truly was a dead-end.

"Is the party out here or what?"

Sandra looked up as a woman in jeans and cowboy boots stepped through the doorway. Piercing blue eyes that missed nothing swept over Sandra.

"I wanted to meet Cory's new friend before you scared her off with one of your horrible stories about birthing horses," Nelda said to the newcomer.

"You don't birth a horse."

"I know. I know." Nelda waved her hand and said to Sandra, "Since Cory seems to have lost all the manners I worked so hard to teach her, let me introduce . . ."

"JJ Garrison," Cory cut in, interrupting Nelda. Everyone turned to her in surprise.

Sandra reached to shake JJ's hand. "Nice to meet you. I'm Sandra Ta . . ."

"Smith," Cory said abruptly.

"Woman, what is wrong with you?" Nelda asked, giving Cory a puzzled look.

Frowning, Sandra watched her. Why had Cory lied about her name?

Cory shrugged. "Nothing. Let's go sit down." When she reached the living room, she suddenly stopped.

"Sandra, can you help me in the kitchen please?" Sandra excused herself and followed Cory. "Are you all right?" Sandra asked when the kitchen door swung closed behind them.

"No. Yes. I'm a little nervous, I guess." She sat the wine on the counter.

"Why did you change my name?"

"Nelda's an architectural buff. She will recognize your name in a heartbeat. It would make it rather awkward why you're working for me. Don't you think?"

Sandra nodded, grateful for Cory's intervention.

Cory fidgeted. "Listen. There's something else I need to ask. I'm not sure how to do it."

"Just ask."

"It may sound weird."

"All right."

"Have you ever been married or changed your name for any reason?"

"No."

"Please, don't lie to me. Tate is your legal birth name?"

"Yes," Sandra answered, confused by Cory's insistence.

Cory hugged her arms across her stomach. "Do you have an ID on you? I mean a photo ID or something?"

Sandra felt as though she had been slapped. She removed her wallet and handed Cory her driver's license. "Will this do?"

Cory read it carefully and looked from the photo to Sandra before handing it back.

"Do you believe me now?" Sandra's irritation seeped into her voice.

"Yes."

"Okay, you two. Enough nookie. I'm starving," Nelda said, sailing into the room. "Cory, get the fish in the oven while I finish the salad. Sandra, can you cook?"

"No. Save me for the dishes." She tried to keep her voice steady. Cory's doubts had hurt. *You brought it on yourself. You started the lies*, she reminded herself.

"Oh, darling," Nelda cried. "You'll do the dishes! I love you already! Go keep JJ company. If you don't feel like talking, just mention horses or jewelry and she'll go non-stop for hours."

Sandra went back into the living room to find JJ deeply engrossed in the blueprints Cory had been looking at in the diner. "Beautiful house, isn't it?" Sandra's irritation melted as she studied the house plans.

JJ looked up at Sandra over a pair of reading glasses. "From what I can tell from this photo, it looks like it needs to be condemned."

"It's not really in bad shape. Cory says the foundation is sound. She's adhering to the original floor plan, so there wouldn't be a lot of demolition and rebuilding." Sandra was pointing to the blueprints.

"It looks like a bunch of lines with boxes and squiggles to me," JJ said with a grimace that caused Sandra to laugh. "How do you know so much about this stuff?"

Sandra shrugged and put the blueprints down. "I picked it up here and there."

JJ was staring at Sandra's ring. When she saw Sandra notice her scrutiny she said, "Nice ring. Was it a gift?"

"No," Sandra replied. "I bought it years ago." The ring had been a gift to herself. She had purchased it after completing her first major project. She sat on the couch. Not wanting the conversation to dwell on her, she took Nelda's advice. "Nelda said to ask you about horses or jewelry."

"Nelda's a horse's butt, but we won't tell her I said so." JJ's eyes sparkled at the mention of Nelda's name.

Sandra felt warmed by the love she saw reflected in JJ's eyes as she spoke of Nelda.

"How long have you two been together?" Sandra asked.

"She first kissed me thirty-four years ago."

Sandra felt her jaw drop. "God. I wasn't sure it was possible for a relationship to last that long."

"Almost anything's possible if you want it bad enough."

"And you wanted it, I guess," Sandra teased.

"With every breath in my body." She seemed to drift off in thought. "So, what's going on between you and Cory?" she asked suddenly.

Sandra blushed and scratched her chin. "Nothing."

"Then why did she invite us up for dinner? We're only invited for dinner on such short notice when she's having a serious trauma. And then you show up, so you must be the reason."

Sandra found it hard to be offended by the woman's bluntness. "I think she feels sorry for me. I'm new to San Antonio."

"Where are you from originally?"

"All over. There are not many cities in Texas I haven't lived in.

"Ever been outside Texas?"

"I spent a few years on the East Coast."

"Cold got to you, didn't it? True Texans can't take that cold."

Sandra laughed. "Tell me about your horses."

JJ's eyes sparkled as she launched into a long detailed explanation of the quarter horses she raised and trained.

Enjoying her enthusiasm, Sandra sat back to listen.

"See, I told you she wouldn't shut up," Nelda quipped as she came in.

"Oh, hush, old woman. I've found someone who knows a muzzle from a fetter."

Nelda looked at Sandra, horrified. "Please. Not another horse lover."

JJ stood and put her arm around Nelda. "Think of it this way, darling. When Sandra's around, I can talk to her about horses and not bother you."

Nelda turned to Sandra. "Honey, how do you feel about adoption? I'll give you a signed contract good for the rest of my life."

"Which is going to be short if you don't stop nagging me," JJ threatened, squeezing Nelda's arm tenderly.

"Look at the gratitude I get for coming to tell you dinner's ready," Nelda grumbled.

"It's a good thing. Sandra and I were about to parch in here with nothing to drink," JJ said, as she walked to Sandra and threw an arm around her shoulders.

Sandra saw Nelda frown as she gazed at them. "Have we met before?" Nelda asked, still staring at Sandra.

"I don't think so. I'm new to San Antonio," Sandra explained.

Nelda started to speak, but Cory calling them from the dining room stopped her.

Sandra liked Cory's house. It was a hodgepodge of furniture carefully selected to blend without screaming perfection. Cory would have made a great interior designer. The house had the same comfortable feel as Laura's home. Cory and Laura could be friends. The thought pleased Sandra.

"Sit wherever you want," Cory instructed them from the side board where she was fussing with the wine.

Sandra moved toward her. "Can I help?" she asked. Cory seemed nervous. "What's wrong?" Sandra asked, reaching for Cory's hand.

"Nothing. Go ahead and take your seat."

Sandra did as instructed. Dinner was comprised of baked fish, a creamy pasta dish, and broccoli. It smelled delicious. They began to eat. An awkward silence seemed to fall over the table. She remembered that Nelda had told her to ask JJ about jewelry.

"I understand you have an interest in jewelry," Sandra said to JJ.

"JJ is a jewelry designer," Cory said.

"Do you specialize in anything in particular?" Sandra asked.

"I'll make any kind of jewelry, but I prefer designing rings."

"JJ has sold her jewelry all over the United States," Nelda informed Sandra proudly. Again, Sandra felt the love pass between the two women.

"And Nelda spreads her fame," Cory said, reaching across the table and squeezing Nelda's hand. Sandra glanced away quickly, confused by her pangs of jealousy.

"I'll have to look for your work the next time I'm out," Sandra said, turning her attention to JJ.

"Actually, you're already acquainted with it," Nelda replied.

Sandra shook her head. "Sorry, I don't believe so, but I'm not much for jewelry."

"What Nelda's rather *rudely* trying to tell you is I designed the ring you're wearing," JJ said, throwing Nelda a sharp glance of disapproval.

Sandra gaped at the ring on her finger. "I purchased this several years ago in New York."

She saw the looks the other three exchanged, and remembered how much she had paid for the ring. It would take her about two and a half years to pay for it on her current dishwasher's salary.

Cory began to nervously push the fish around on her plate.

"Sandra was telling me she loves to ride horses," JJ said, breaking the awkward silence. "Cory, since Sandra is off Monday and Tuesday, and you're the boss and can take off whenever you like, why don't the two of you come down next

Monday and spend the night with us? We can go riding and maybe work in a little night fishing. The rest will do you good."

Cory started to speak, but JJ cut her off by directing her attention to Sandra. "Do you like to fish, Sandra?"

"I've never tried it," she admitted.

"Never been fishing! Lord, woman, there's probably a Communist plot lurking there somewhere," Nelda exclaimed.

"So it's settled," JJ said, slapping the table.

Sandra smiled, liking these women. The rest of the meal passed in small talk about the unpredictability of the Texas weather.

Afterwards, Sandra and JJ cleaned up the kitchen while Cory and Nelda broke out the Scrabble game and opened another bottle of wine. The evening slipped away much too quickly for Sandra. She put off leaving as long as she politely could.

Hours later back in her motel room, Sandra sank into her bed with an odd sense of contentment. *Maybe I should move down here*, she thought as she drifted off to sleep.

CHAPTER FOURTEEN

Sandra found herself caught between conflicting desires. She longed for the week to be over so that she and Cory could head for Rockport. At the same time, every minute slipping by was one less in which she might be able to get even a glimpse of Cory. Since the night of the dinner, Cory seemed to be deliberately avoiding her.

As Sandra's early shift was ending on Friday, Wilma the heavy-set cook came in shaking her head.

"What's wrong with you?" Maria asked as she stirred a large pot of soup.

"Anna told me Cory got a call from her realtor. Seems some land investors are looking at her dream house. They want the property to build a subdivision."

"That means they'll tear the old house down," Sandra moaned. She felt a deep sense of loss for the stately old home. "Cory must be devastated."

"Yeah," Wilma said with a sigh. "Either way the boss has lost it. She's sick with disappointment." She shook her head wistfully. "Sure wish I had the money. I'd buy it for her myself. I ain't never seen anybody want something so bad."

Sandra hung up her apron. "I'll see you two later." She left the diner through the back door and went to her bike. The loss of the house would devastate Cory. Sandra sat on her bike, gently revving the motor. It was wrong for Cory to lose her dream home. One of the things that Sandra admired most about Cory was her tenacity. Being a business owner herself, she knew how hard Cory worked. She knew the stress and heartache that went hand-in-hand with owning your own business. That house was meant for Cory.

Sandra considered her options. She could offer to loan the money to Cory, but she'd never take it. Or she could buy the property and sell it to her at a price Cory could afford, but somehow she didn't think Cory would see the act as anything but charity. Or she could buy the house herself. Sandra smiled and went back into the diner for a phone book.

Twenty minutes later, she was in her room calling Allison. She gave her the realtor's name and number.

"I don't care what you have to pay," she instructed. "Pull every string necessary. If things aren't moving fast enough, call in a few favors, but close the deal today before those investors get wind of it. Buy it through Lone Star Construction. I don't want it to be common knowledge that I'm the buyer."

"This must be some place," Allison said. "You aren't planning on moving to San Antonio, are you?"

"No. It's an investment."

Sandra could barely contain her excitement. The evening shift seemed to drag out forever. Cory's loss affected everyone at the diner. The tension exploded when Ginny dropped a steak dinner.

The sound of shattering porcelain startled Sandra.

"Damn," Ginny shrieked. "Maria, the plate was too hot. Don't sit them so close to the stove."

"Stop being so clumsy," Maria snapped back. "I've got enough to do without having to re-do the order because you can't hold onto the plate."

"It was too hot," Ginny complained.

"Should I buy you some gloves to protect those soft little hands of yours?"

Before Ginny could counter, Cory stormed through the kitchen door.

"What's going on in here?" she said in a harsh whisper. "I can hear you two all the way to the front door." Without waiting for an answer, she grabbed two orders from the warming tray. "Ginny, get these orders out there now."

"Those are Anna's," Ginny protested.

"I don't give a rat's ass if they belong to the King of Siam, get them out there now!"

Shocked by Cory's outburst, Ginny, Maria, and Sandra all stared. Their shocked silence seemed to penetrate Cory's anger.

She took a deep breath and sat the plates down. "I'm sorry. I'm tired. I'll take the plates out myself, Ginny. You have enough to do with your own stations."

Ginny ran forward and gave Cory a quick hug before Cory could pick the plates up again.

"Go to your office and lie down for a while," Ginny prompted. "You know Maria and I are all bluff. We can handle things. Right guys?" She turned to Maria and Sandra for confirmation.

"Sure we can. Ginny and I were only blowing off steam. You know she thinks I'm the world's greatest cook," Maria teased, winking at Ginny.

"Just like Maria knows I'm the world's greatest waitress," Ginny teased back.

"Yeah," Sandra called, joining in the banter. "And everyone knows I'm the world's greatest dishwasher."

At that, the other three women turned to her as one and burst out laughing.

"I think we all need to get back to work," Cory said, shaking her head. Without waiting for a response she took Anna's orders and headed back into the dining room.

Ginny gave Maria a quick wink. "I need another T-bone, rare with a dry potato."

Maria tossed the steak on the grill. "I need a pitcher of margaritas and a foot massage."

Anna swung through the door calling out, "I need a number seven and three specials."

The crisis blew over. Sandra went back to her piles of dirty dishes, but not before she sent up a small prayer that Allison would not run into any major roadblocks. In all her years in business, she had never wanted a deal to close so badly as she did this one.

By the time Sandra arrived at work for the dinner shift the following evening, the deal had closed. The deed had been air expressed down to her and was now in her motel room. The house and property had cost more than market value, but to Sandra, it was well worth every penny.

The staff was moving about, quietly preparing for the dinner rush. "Did someone die?" Sandra asked Anna, meaning it as a joke. She had tried to avoid Anna after that first night, but tonight she felt too good.

Anna did not bother looking up from the napkins she was folding. "May as well have. Someone bought Cory's house today."

"That's too bad," Sandra said, struggling to keep the excitement out of her voice. "How's Cory?"

"How do you think she feels?" Anna growled. She slammed a silverware setting inside a napkin and wrapped it furiously. "Damn, it's not fair. I hate those bastards!"

Sandra flinched at her bitterness and started toward the office. "She doesn't want to see anyone," Anna snapped.

"I need to talk to her."

"I said, she doesn't want to see anyone, and that includes you."

Sandra knew Anna's inability to help Cory was causing her aggression, but she wanted to talk to Cory. "I'll only be a minute."

"Get in the kitchen and do the dishes you were hired to do," Anna ordered. "You aren't going in there. She's been hurt enough already." Anna rose from the table. Ginny and Louise joined them.

"I wasn't asking you for your permission," Sandra shot back. Anna's attitude was taking the fun out of her accomplishment.

Anna started toward Sandra, but Louise stepped between them. "Stop it. Both of you. We'll have customers any minute, and Cory doesn't need this." She pointed to the napkins Anna had been folding. "Please, take those to your station and cool off."

Anna reluctantly stepped away and grabbed up the tray she had been working on. Ginny went to help her.

Louise turned to Sandra. "Don't let Anna bother you. She's just so frustrated about not being able to help Cory. Hell, we all are. Cory has done so much for all of us." She took a deep breath and shook her head. "If you really need to talk to her go ahead, but if you make matters worse by going in there and talking about the house, I'll personally kick your butt."

Sandra stared at her, shocked. She had considered Louise to be a rather mousy, spineless thing. *Was I ever wrong*, she admitted to herself.

The door opened and a family of five walked in. "Everyone to work," Louise said with her normal cheery smile in place.

Sandra abandoned her trip to see Cory and headed for the kitchen. Her thoughts of seeing Cory were soon lost in the dinner hour rush.

Cory came by an hour or so later and spoke with Wilma and Maria. Sandra saw her hesitate before coming over to her. "Louise said you needed to talk to me. I'm going home now. Is there something you need before I go?"

I need to tell you I love you and want to hold you and make all of your pain disappear, Sandra wanted to say, but could only shake her head. "It can wait."

Cory stepped closer. "Sandra, about this weekend."

"Go with me on my bike."

Cory stared at her, horrified. "Not on your life," she said.

"It'll be fun."

"I'm not going," Cory confessed, turning her head to avoid meeting Sandra's gaze.

"Why?"

Cory shrugged. "I wouldn't be very good company."

"Is it because of the house?"

A look a pain crossed Cory's face. "Partly."

"Am I the other reason?" Sandra managed to ask around the knot building up in her throat.

Cory stared at the floor.

"Would it make any difference if I weren't leaving after next week?"

Cory looked up.

Was that a look of hope that flashed in her eyes? Sandra wondered.

"Is that an option?" Cory asked.

Sandra gave the thought a moment of consideration. What would need to be done to move her office to San Antonio? Maybe she should expand, leave the main office in Dallas and let Allison run it. Allison had more than proven herself capable.

"I thought not," Cory said and sighed, taking Sandra's hesitation wrong. She started to turn away.

"Come with me this weekend," Sandra pleaded.

"It'll only make it harder," Cory hissed, looking up to find Wilma and Maria watching them. "Look, let's talk about this tomorrow. The whole place has enough to gossip about already," Cory said.

"They're concerned about you because they care. They would do anything for you. Can I come by tonight after work?"

"No. That's not a good idea."

"If the lights are on, I'm stopping, and I'd like to stay," Sandra persisted. She swallowed, trying to keep her voice from shaking. She could not believe she was pushing so hard.

Cory's eyes blazed, but not before Sandra saw the glint of desire in them. "You can drive by all you want, but the lights won't be on." Without waiting for a reply, she turned and stalked out.

Sandra concentrated on the piles of dirty dishes. Tonight she intended to be out of here on time. In her haste, she dropped and shattered four plates before her shift was over.

Wilma shook her head as she was getting out her purse to leave. "You two better work it out soon," she said. "We're running out of dishes."

"There's nothing to work out," Sandra admitted. "I don't think she's interested in even trying to see if something might be there. Besides, I'm beginning to get the impression everyone would be happier if I left."

"Ah, you've been listening to Anna. She's crazy with jealousy. She has been head-over-heels in love with Cory for years. Can't you see that?" Wilma found her car keys and slung her purse over her shoulder. "You know when I first saw you I told myself that you were way too smart to be working here. But the more I know you, the more goose-shit green you get. You can't see what's right before your nose."

167

"Like what?"

Wilma rolled her eyes and stalked off mumbling.

Sandra was so nervous she was nauseous. She rode slowly to Cory's and sat in the driveway staring at the darkened house. She considered ringing the doorbell, but Cory had made it clear she was not welcome. After several minutes, she pulled away and headed for her empty motel room.

Cory failed to show at the diner on Sunday and the day passed agonizingly slow for Sandra. She considered calling Nelda and JJ and canceling the trip to see them, but changed her mind as she stepped out into the warm April night air.

She would be going back to Dallas in a week, and work would again claim her life. She wanted one more free weekend. She went to her motel room long enough to shower and pack. It was almost midnight when she climbed onto her bike and roared toward Rockport.

Not wanting to arrive at the crack of dawn, Sandra went to Port Aransas and crossed the ferry during the wee hours of the morning. Parking on the beach, she sat in sand beside her bike. The sounds of the waves gradually eased the tension from her neck and shoulders. The wind blew away her pain and confusion. She simply sat, not allowing herself to feel anything other than the warm night air settling around her like a soothing hand.

Along with the first hint of light in the east came the shrieking of the gulls. Plovers and killdeers scurried to the water's edge in search of breakfast. Shrimp boats bobbed on the distant horizon.

Sandra stood and stretched, watching the sun tint the sky pink. As she watched the early rays glint across the water, she made a decision. She would have the deed to the house transferred into Cory's name and leave it in her office next Sunday night before she left to return to Dallas. By the time Cory found it, Sandra would be gone.

Sandra refused to think about how life would be without Cory. Her eyes burned from sleeplessness. Her body felt bruised and sore. Numb with heartache, she climbed onto her bike. She had loved Carol in the beginning, but never with the intensity she felt for Cory.

Sandra threw back her head and closed her eyes against the pain. "I'd give everything I own just to hear her say she loves me one time," she whispered to the roaring tide.

CHAPTER FIFTEEN

It was noon before Sandra rode up the lane to Nelda and JJ's ranch. Her heart skipped a beat at the sight of Cory's car. She had come after all!

"There you are," Nelda called as the three of them came around the house. "We were about to give up on you."

"I got a late start," Sandra lied, trying not to look at Cory. Nelda and JJ gave her a quick hug, while Cory stood several feet away.

JJ examined Sandra's bike. "You sure have expensive tastes for a dishwasher," she remarked, eyeing Sandra.

Too tired to continue the charade, Sandra decided they

could either accept her or go to hell. "I'm not normally a dishwasher."

Cory's head shot up and gave a small shake. She seemed to be trying to warn Sandra, but Sandra was too tired to care.

"Nooo!" JJ exclaimed sarcastically.

"I didn't do anything wrong. I was going to be in San Antonio for a few weeks and wanted something to do." The reason sounded lame and stupid.

"So you got a job washing dishes?" JJ asked, rocking on her heels.

"She's slumming," Cory snapped.

Sandra stepped toward her, intending to verbally defend herself, but JJ grabbed her arm.

"Take me for a spin. I've always wanted to ride one of these things."

Sandra hesitated.

"Come on," JJ urged and hopped on. She patted the seat in front of her. "Hurry up or I may want to drive. We'll meet you two at the barn in an hour," JJ called to the others. "Nelda, bring the lunches we packed."

Sandra slapped her leg and stormed back to the bike. "Here," she said, handing JJ the extra helmet before yanking on her own. "Hold on," she snapped as the machine sprang to life. They roared down the lane to the highway, leaving a trail of dust.

JJ tapped her on the shoulder and pointed to a road coming up. Sandra continued to follow JJ's tapped-out directions until they turned onto a narrow road riddled with potholes. She eased the throttle back and cruised down the road that led to a small sandy stretch of beach.

"Stop here!" JJ yelled over the engine.

Sandra killed the engine.

"Come on," JJ said and led the way. They walked a short distance across the sand and through a small grove of trees.

As they emerged from the trees, Sandra's breath caught at the beauty of the cove before them.

"I like to come here when I need to think," JJ explained, sitting on the sand and folding her feet beneath her. "Things aren't going very well between you and Cory, are they?"

Sandra stretched out beside her. "They aren't going at all," she admitted.

"She's scared. There's too much about you she doesn't know."

"Why can't she take me for what I am now?"

"Because, that's not who you really are."

"You don't seem to be having a problem with it," Sandra said, staring up at the older woman.

"I'm not in love with you," JJ responded bluntly.

Sandra was left without a retort. JJ didn't know Cory as well as she thought if she believed that.

JJ traced patterns in the sand with her finger. "Cory has a tendency to take in strays."

Sandra started to rise, but JJ placed a hand on her shoulder and stopped her. "I'm not calling you a stray, so don't get a burr up your butt. Cory's got a mothering complex or something. Haven't you noticed how she's always trying to help someone?"

Sandra thought about how Cory gave Anna rides to work. Sandra handed out meals to any homeless person who knocked at the kitchen door. She donated the leftover food from the restaurant to a local shelter. Sandra relaxed and nodded.

"Four years ago she hired a woman to paint the diner," JJ explained. "They got involved and the woman moved in with her. Three months later, she skipped town with practically every penny Cory had. Cory almost lost the diner. That financial setback cost her the house she wanted. I guess you know the house sold to an out of town firm last week."

Sandra eyed her to see if she suspected anything, but JJ

seemed to be simply relating the facts. "Do you think I'm after her money?"

JJ looked at her for a long moment, and shook her head. "No. I think you could probably buy everything Cory owns and not blink an eye."

Guilty as charged, Sandra looked away.

"I thought so," JJ snorted. Sandra's actions had confirmed her suspicions. "Who are you anyway?"

Sandra sighed and brushed her hair from her face. "Nobody really. The whole thing seems pretty silly now." She trickled sand between her fingers. "My doctor suggested I get away for awhile and rest."

"And you decided washing dishes was rest?" JJ asked incredulously.

"I took the job to be near Cory, but in the long run it worked. I'm too busy to think while I'm working, and too tired to think when I'm not."

JJ nodded. "I can understand that."

"JJ," Sandra said as she sat up. "I love her and I swear I'd never intentionally do anything to hurt her."

JJ blinked and looked away. "Unfortunately, it's the people we love the most who we normally hurt the most, and it's never intentional."

"So I should leave and let her get on with her life?"

"Once you leave, you can never go back. The loss will hurt you a little more every year."

"Sounds like the voice of experience." Sandra took JJ's hand.

JJ turned to her. Sandra was surprised to see tears. "I walked away from something that meant more than life itself to me, and I've never stopped regretting it."

"Why did you leave?"

"I let someone convince me I was doing the right thing. That my leaving would be best."

"And it wasn't?"

Instead of answering, JJ looked at her watch and hopped up. "We need to get back or we'll be late."

After meeting Nelda and Cory at the barn, they spent the rest of the afternoon riding over the sixty acres Nelda and JJ owned. The tension between Sandra and Cory eased as the day progressed. By the time they left to go fishing that night, everyone was in high spirits. They piled the gear into the bed of Nelda and JJ's truck. Sandra and Cory squeezed into the small rear seat. Nelda drove a few miles beyond the cove where JJ and Sandra had talked earlier in the afternoon. Sandra wondered what it was that JJ had given up. Her musing was cut short by the truck stopping.

"We'll meet back here in three hours," JJ said as they unloaded the fishing gear.

Cory checked her watch. "All right."

"Why are we splitting up?" Sandra asked as she and Cory set off in the opposite direction from JJ and Nelda.

"Nelda is convinced that the fish can smell people. She swears she's never caught anything when she's been fishing with more than one person." Cory laughed. "I think it's an excuse to sneak off in the dark with JJ. You watch. They won't have a single fish when they come back, but they'll both be smiling."

Sandra laughed. "I think it's great they love each other so much. I can't imagine ever finding someone who would love me like that."

The statement hung awkwardly between them as they walked out to a short pier. Sandra stopped to look at the night sky flooded with stars. "It's so beautiful," she murmured. "A billion pinpoints of light." She closed her eyes and let the salt-laden air embrace her. A breeze tickled the loose tendrils of hair around her face. Sandra let her imagination flow. The wind became Cory's hands. Her face was caressed with the

174

softest of touches, and warm whispers of air trailed along her arms.

Cory's voice jarred her from her fantasy. "Let's fish off the end of the pier," Cory said, leading the way.

A large light was positioned to point its bright illumination out into the water, while providing only a soft glow on the pier.

"Bring your pole over here. I'll show you how to rig your line," Cory instructed.

Sandra did as asked. She stood by and watched as Cory unsnapped a small brass object tied on the line.

"This is a swivel. It makes it easier to switch back and forth between an artificial lure or a hook for bait," Cory explained. As she turned to show Sandra, a gust of wind caught the line and pulled it from Cory's hand. They reached for it at the same time and their hands touched.

Sandra gasped as a flame of desire shot through her. She captured Cory's hand within hers. "Stop pushing me away," she whispered. "I love you. I'll tell you anything you want to know. I'll move anywhere you want to live. I'll spend the rest of my life washing dishes, but please don't push me away."

Cory's free hand slid around Sandra's neck and pulled her into an urgent kiss. Sandra dropped the pole she held, ignoring its crashing clatter to the pier, and pulled Cory into her arms.

Cory broke the kiss and hugged Sandra tightly, "So help me God, if you're lying to me, I'll track you to the ends of the earth," she sobbed as she clung to Sandra.

"I'm not lying," Sandra promised, blinking away the tears that burned her eyes. "I love you," she whispered into Cory's ear. Sandra shivered as Cory's hands slid under her shirt and caressed her bare breasts.

"I've wanted to do this since practically the first moment I saw you," Cory moaned. The sound caused Sandra's nipples to tighten more.

"Let's not waste anymore time," Sandra pleaded as her

lips moved across Cory's throat. She pulled Cory down to the pier. "Ouch," Sandra yelped as a splinter bit into her knee. They pulled apart and began to laugh. "This always works in the movies," Sandra grumbled.

"The sand will be worse," Cory predicted. "Nelda and JJ won't be back to the truck for three hours."

The abandoned fishing tackle was quickly retrieved before they raced back to the truck. They pitched the gear into the truck bed. Sandra caught Cory and kissed her hungrily. "I've never made love in a vehicle before," she said, pulling open the door and climbing in.

"I'm glad they didn't lock the doors," Cory said, scrambling in behind Sandra and closing the door. The sounds of the night disappeared once they were inside the truck. Sandra froze as a wave of insecurity crashed over her. She wanted to make Cory happy. She wanted to be the greatest lover Cory had ever known, but little pins of doubt began to pierce her confidence. Carol's cruel jabs came back and threatened to puncture her courage.

Sandra's heart pounded in her ears. She was on the verge of leaping from the truck when Cory's hand brushed against her hair.

"You're so beautiful," Cory breathed as she continued to brush Sandra's hair away from her face.

Peace embraced Sandra like a lover's arms. She looked into Cory's eyes and felt an enormous surge of love and courage. "I want to make you happy," Sandra said.

"Then make love to me," Cory said as her hands tugged at Sandra's shirt.

Their clothes scattered across the truck in their haste. Sandra pulled Cory beneath her and covered her face and throat with kisses. Her blood pounded with a lust as ancient as time when Cory ground her pelvis against Sandra's leg.

Sandra captured a straining nipple and sucked it into her mouth. Her head was caught between Cory's hands and urged downward. Sandra slid farther down the seat, her legs bent in

176

order to reach her goal. She grabbed Cory's hips as they rose to meet her mouth. The delicious musky scent of desire fueled Sandra's actions.

Sandra was convinced nothing could be more powerful than the sense of smell. How could anything be more provocative? And then her tongue dipped into Cory's wetness. Silky flesh surrounded her tongue as a delicate saltiness teased her taste buds. Cory was the tide, Sandra the moon. She pulled Cory deep into her mouth before releasing her hold to send Cory crashing back.

Driven by Cory's cries of pleasure, Sandra feasted on Cory's desire like a woman dying of starvation. The truck rocked wildly with their lovemaking. Needing to feel more of her, Sandra slipped two fingers into Cory's wetness while her tongue continued its banquet of rapture.

Sandra felt Cory stiffen in anticipation and she narrowed her concentration to the delicate point against the tip of her tongue. She held her breath as Cory's body was racked by a tremor that escalated into a wild thrashing. Sandra fought to hang on. Sandra's ears filled with Cory's cries of release, while her shoulders became prisoners of Cory's long legs.

Unable and unwilling to give up the pleasure she was experiencing, Sandra continued to stroke Cory with her tongue until a second orgasm engulfed her. She tried to protest as Cory pulled her up into her arms.

"I want you now," Cory said, her voice shaky and thick with desire. "Sit up," she insisted as she knelt on the floor. She spread Sandra's legs. "Brace them on the dash," she said, pushing Sandra's legs up. "I want access to everything," she insisted, lowering her head between Sandra's legs and gently nipping the insides of her thighs. Her hands slipped beneath Sandra's hips and pulled her to the edge of the seat.

Cory's tongue slipped between Sandra's cheeks and gently rotated. The sensation was overwhelming. Sandra bit down on her lip to keep from crying out. Not even Dee had shown her this. Cory's left thumb began a light feather stroke over

Sandra's swollen desire as the fingers of her right hand began a gentle rhythm in and out of Sandra. Cory's tongue and thumb created an inferno within Sandra like none she had ever known.

Sandra thrashed as her body melted into Cory's mouth and hands. She begged for release, but Cory kept her hanging at the edge. After what seemed an eternity, Sandra felt herself slipping into a state of total awareness. The feel of Cory's hands and tongue intensified until she could no longer distinguish which was what.

"Please."

She heard her voice from a distance. The pressure of Cory's touch shifted slightly, and Sandra's world exploded. Never had Sandra felt such an urgent need. Her hands locked onto the back of the seat as she screamed out Cory's name. She felt the cool glass of the windshield against the bottom of her feet. She gave in to the sensations and let her body be consumed by Cory's fire.

CHAPTER SIXTEEN

Sandra heard Cory's voice far away from the warm fuzzy place where she now floated. She tried to speak, but it was too much effort. Cory's voice took on an edge of panic. Sandra fought her way back to see why. She forced her eyes open and found Cory dressed and leaning over her.

"Thank God," Cory breathed loudly. "Are you all right?"

"I think I've been screwed to death," Sandra managed to moan.

"Don't make fun. I've been trying to rouse you for five minutes. I was about to start yelling for Nelda and JJ. What the hell happened?"

Sandra could see the concern on her face and pulled her into her arms. "I love you," she declared, holding Cory close.

"I love you too," Cory said, pulling back and gazing into Sandra's eyes. "Are you all right?"

"I've never been better." Sandra smiled foolishly, reveling in Cory's declaration of love.

Cory kissed her softly. "You'd better get dressed. It's almost time for Nelda and JJ to return."

"Already! They said three hours."

"Which is only a few minutes from now," Cory informed her.

Sandra sat up, still feeling shaky.

"Let me help you." With Cory's help Sandra managed to get dressed.

"We'd better open the doors," Cory said and giggled. "Nelda has a nose like a bloodhound. She'll know exactly what we've been up to."

Sandra was sitting on the running board with Cory leaning against the truck when Nelda and JJ returned. "They won't have a single fish," Cory whispered to Sandra.

"How did you do?" Cory called to them.

"No luck," Nelda answered, much too cheerfully for someone who had spent three fruitless hours fishing. "How about you two?"

"Nothing but a few nibbles," Cory answered, smiling suggestively down at Sandra.

"Really?" JJ asked, surprised. Nelda cleared her throat and JJ added lamely, "Guess this was just a bad night for fishing. Maybe it will be better next time, Sandra."

Cory and Sandra exchanged amused looks before climbing into the back seat.

The four women rode in companionable silence. They were already on the main highway leading to the ranch before they met a car. The oncoming car's headlights illuminated the truck's windshield.

JJ leaned forward. "Nelda, what's this on the windshield?"

"What's it look like?" Nelda asked.

JJ peered at the image. "It looks like a footprint!"

Sandra felt her face flame, remembering the feel of the cool windshield against the bottom of her feet.

"How did a footprint get on the windshield?" JJ asked, puzzled.

Nelda chuckled.

"What's so funny?" JJ insisted, staring at her.

"I guess it was a fine night for fishing after all, sweetheart."

"What do you mean it was . . . oh." She stopped and threw a glance over her shoulder at Cory who was intently studying the darkness outside her window.

"Mighty fine night indeed," Sandra agreed and squeezed Cory's hand as they all burst out laughing.

Sandra woke to the feel of Cory's soft breasts pressed against her back. "Are you planning on sleeping all day, sleepyhead?" Cory asked, nuzzling Sandra's neck.

"Considering the fact that I got no sleep last night, the thought does sound appealing." She turned onto her back. "But who needs sleep?" She pulled Cory on top of her and gazed into her eyes. "There are so many things I want to do with you," she said, caressing Cory's back.

"Can we start with what you're doing right now?"

"Only if you promise to describe in great detail exactly what it is I'm doing."

Cory leaned forward, her husky voice tickling Sandra's ear. "You're making me very wet and very horny." Her tongue teased Sandra's ear.

"I can do something about that." Pulling Cory's legs to either side of her body, Sandra wiggled down until her head was between Cory's legs. Resting her head on a pillow she drove her tongue into Cory's wetness. She suppressed a groan of excitement when Cory braced her arms against the wall and began to rhythmically rub her desire against Sandra's face.

Sandra lost track of everything but the feel of Cory.

The smell of fresh coffee and bacon finally lured them from the bedroom. The large country kitchen held a warm comfortable atmosphere Sandra had longed for in her own home, but never managed to achieve. As they chatted, she began to realize it was not the house providing the warmth, but rather the love and friendship within the house. Their conversation gradually turned to JJ's jewelry.

"Do you work out of the house?" Sandra asked.

"I have a small shop set up in the back. I'll give you the nickel tour later, if you'd like to see it."

"That would be great."

They finished breakfast and cleaned the kitchen together. "We still have time for another horseback ride if you'd like," Nelda offered. Everyone agreed.

"Why don't we go out the back way and show Sandra the shop. We can go to the barn from there," JJ offered.

Nelda led the way down the long hallway. Cory and Sandra brought up the rear, sneaking a quick kiss.

Nelda gave Sandra a run-down on the house's history. "The house was built in the early forties by a retired banker. There were rumors he was a gangster from Chicago and he moved out here to live his last few years in peace. Of course, people being the suspicious, greedy souls they are, thought he had hidden tons of loot out here somewhere. After he died, a lot of damage was done to the house by people trying to find his hidden money."

Sandra saw a flash of disappointment cross Cory's face and knew she was thinking of the house she thought she had lost. Sandra felt a warm glow in knowing she would be able to give it to her.

Nelda opened the door to JJ's workshop.

"This is it," JJ said with pride in her voice.

Sandra was greeted by a variety of pleasant smells she could not identify. A quick glance showed her a room full of color and plants. She looked with approval at the bay window that allowed light to pour in.

"My eyes aren't what they used to be," JJ admitted, seeing Sandra observing the window. "We had the window put in a few years ago."

"It's a fantastic room," Sandra marveled, looking around. "No wonder you're able to create such beautiful jewelry. I could . . ." She stopped short. The blood rushed from her head so quickly she staggered. Cory and Nelda helped her into a wooden chair JJ had pulled from her desk. A thousand thoughts ran through Sandra's mind as memories from childhood rushed to overtake her. Could it really be?

"Sandra?" Cory said as she hovered beside her.

Sandra pushed her gently to the side and stood. She removed the faded photo of herself and Mr. Peepers from her wallet and compared the photo to the bear on the shelf. "Mr. Peepers," she croaked. "It's Mr. Peepers." She pointed to the battered old bear with a plaid vest and an odd shaped hat that sat over one ear.

A strangled cry came from behind her, and Nelda grabbed JJ as JJ's knees buckled.

"What the hell's going on?" Nelda's scared voice demanded.

"Mr. Peepers." Sandra could not stop repeating the bear's name. Time stood still for her as she rose and made her way to the tattered old bear.

"My God," Nelda gasped when Sandra picked up the bear and clutched it to her heart.

Realization began to penetrate Sandra's shock of seeing the bear sitting on the shelf. She turned and stared into the deep blue eyes that were so much like her own.

"How did you get my bear?" she managed to ask as JJ slowly pulled away from Nelda.

"It can't be," JJ whispered, walking as though her feet were weighed down with stones. She took the photo from Sandra's hand and looked at it. "After all those years of looking and hoping. You're my Sandra. My baby girl."

"Mother." Sandra's body moved to the woman she had been led to believe abandoned her. She could no longer find the hate she had carried around inside for most of her life. They met in the center of the room facing each other.

Sandra was pale and clinging to the odd-looking bear, while JJ trembled with tears trailing down her cheeks. Nelda and Cory stood to the side, frozen by the mammoth wave of emotions tearing about the room.

For an eternity the mother and daughter stood staring at each other until a strangled, broken sob tore from Sandra's throat.

"My baby, my baby," JJ chanted, pulling a weeping Sandra into her arms.

Nelda touched Cory's arm and they silently left the room, leaving Sandra and JJ to begin repairing the damage caused by thirty-four years of needless separation.

Sandra clutched JJ's hand and listened as JJ told about how they had moved to San Antonio when Sandra was two. JJ met Nelda at the restaurant and fell in love with her. JJ patted the ragged old bear Sandra continued to clutch.

My intuition about the diner was correct, Sandra thought as JJ continued.

"You saw this bear in a department store and wouldn't let go of him. I named him after Nelda's diner." She wiped her tears and took a deep breath. "I had been sneaking around seeing Nelda for several months. Sometimes I'd take you with me, and sometimes I'd leave you with the next door neighbor.

She and I took turns baby-sitting each other's kids. Your father got suspicious and followed me. He caught Nelda and me together," JJ said, shaking her head as if trying to dislodge the memory. "He was so angry. He wouldn't listen to anything I tried to say," she continued. "He filed for a divorce and told the judge I was a lesbian. I lost custody of you. I wasn't allowed to go near you."

JJ went on to explain how she had tried to keep track of them, but her limited funds at the time combined with Sandra and her father's constant moving eventually caused JJ to lose them.

"On your eighteenth birthday, Nelda and I hired a private investigator. He searched for four years before he finally gave up. It's like you simply dropped off the face of the earth." She wiped tears from Sandra's cheek. "But I never completely gave up. To this day, every time I go somewhere the first thing I do is check the phone book for Sandra Garrison."

"Garrison?" Sandra asked, stunned. "My name's Tate."

JJ stared at her horrified before bursting into a fresh batch of tears. "The bastard," she wept. "The low-down dirty bastard! I never dreamed he would change his name. If I had only thought, maybe I could have found you." She grabbed Sandra's hands. "Where were you when you turned eighteen?"

"In Dallas," Sandra said and sniffed.

"So was I," JJ said with a sigh. She rested her head on Sandra's shoulder. "I'll kill him for this."

"He's already dead," Sandra answered, torn with conflicting emotions for her father. He was the only person who had ever truly been there for her. She closed her eyes and fought the anger that threatened when the realization of what his warped sense of love had cost her. So many things fell into place. His working odd jobs. The constant moving from city to city. Even the missing birth certificate, she could never take to school.

JJ raised up. "Honey, for your sake, I'm sorry that he died.

I know this is twice as rough for you." She took Sandra's hand. "I never wanted to leave you. I told him I would give up Nelda if he wouldn't take you from me, but he wouldn't listen." She stared across the room and out the large window. "He was a proud man and felt like I deliberately set out to destroy him."

"I feel as though I should be angry with him, but somehow I can't make myself."

"He was your father. He had his good points. Remember the good times and don't dwell on the past. Nelda taught me to live in the present and to accept the things you can't change. I knew I would never give up looking for you, but I had to let go of the obsession of finding you. Does that make sense?"

Sandra nodded.

Silence fell between them as they sat looking at each other.

"We've got so much to catch up on," JJ said. "We don't even know each other. I want to know everything there is to know about you." She patted Sandra's cheek. They looked around, realizing for the first time that they were alone. JJ stood and took Sandra's hand. "Why don't we go find Nelda and Cory. They're probably frantic by now. They will want to hear this, as well."

They found Nelda and Cory sitting in the living room. Glancing at the tall grandfather clock, Sandra was shocked to see it was already after three. Cory rose and hugged Sandra to her.

"I've found my mother," Sandra sobbed in Cory's ear. "Thank you."

Cory clutched her closer as Nelda held JJ.

"Sandra, I'm sorry I didn't say anything," Cory said. "I knew JJ had been searching for her daughter named Sandra for years. That's why I checked your driver's license and asked about your name at dinner last week. I told them your name was Smith because I was scared. I was afraid to trust you. There were so many things I didn't know about you. I wanted to trust you, but I was so scared." She shook her head and shrugged. "I'm so sorry."

"It's all right," Sandra said, caressing Cory's cheeks. "I understand. Let's sit down."

Cory led Sandra to the couch and sat her between JJ and herself while Nelda settled on the other side of JJ.

"I should have known," Nelda said, turning so she could see everyone. "The first night I met you at Cory's, you looked so familiar. I kept thinking I knew you from somewhere. Now I see it in your eyes. You both have the same color eyes."

"It didn't help any that Sandra and I kept trying to hide her real name," Cory sighed, before stopping suddenly. "Why isn't your name Garrison?"

"He changed their name," JJ supplied.

"I thought your name was Smith," Nelda cut in.

Cory shook her head. "No, I was stupid and told you it was Smith because I was afraid to trust Sandra. I thought there had to be more to the story of why she was here. And, I knew you would recognize her name."

"Well, what is your name?" Nelda demanded, truly confused by now.

"Sandra Tate. I'm from Dallas."

"The *architect*!" Nelda's eyes widened. "But how . . ."

JJ held up her hands. "Why don't I start at the beginning and Sandra can fill in her part of the story as we go along."

JJ and Sandra repeated the story they had only moments before told each other.

It was well after dark before Sandra and Cory left to return to San Antonio. Sandra found herself torn between staying with JJ or returning to San Antonio with Cory. She finally decided to return to San Antonio with Cory. JJ and Nelda would come in as soon as they could arrange for someone to feed the horses for a few days. They would bring Sandra's bike back in their truck.

CHAPTER SEVENTEEN

It was after midnight. Cory and Sandra lay in Cory's bed, unable to sleep.

"We've got a lot to decide," Sandra said, rolling into Cory's arms.

"I've been lying here thinking about that." Cory hesitated. "Sandra, I don't want to sell Peepers."

"I wouldn't ask you to. What would you think about me opening an office here? I can leave Allison in charge of the office in Dallas. She can handle things there as well as I can."

"Would it work?"

Sandra smiled at the excitement in Cory's voice. "I think

so. I want to get back to designing buildings." She rolled to the edge of the bed and turned on the light.

"What are you doing?" Cory asked, blinking against the sudden brightness.

Sandra crawled out of bed and walked naked to her backpack that lay on a chair. She removed the Federal Express envelope and returned to bed. On the way back from Rockport, she had asked Cory to stop at the motel on the pretense of picking up clothes. She sat clutching the envelope to her, suddenly afraid.

"What's that?"

"I bought you something. At the time, I thought I was doing the right thing, but now I don't know. Don't be mad at me, okay?"

Cory sat up in bed. "You silly thing. Why would I be angry with you for buying me something?"

"I only did it because I love you. I couldn't stand to see you hurting. I was going to leave it in your office Sunday night before I left." She gave up explaining and reluctantly handed Cory the envelope.

Cory ran her hand over the envelope without opening it. "Sandra, if this is what I'm thinking it might be, I can't take it."

Sandra felt the cold knot of fear in the pit of her stomach. She sat up on her knees. "Why not?"

"Because I'll never be able to repay you. I don't want you to ever think I only care for you because of your money."

"Cory, stop it. Please, don't do this. I spent eight years with a woman who only stayed because of my money. Trust me when I tell you, I know when people are after my money. We both know how that feels."

Cory looked at her stunned. "Who told you about that?"

"JJ told me. She was right to do so. It made me understand you better. Now please, try to understand me. I've had more money than I've known what to do with since I was in my early thirties, but I've never experienced the kind of love I have for you. Let me give you this," she pleaded, touching the envelope.

Cory blinked away tears. "I don't know what to say."

"Tell me you'll let me use your plans to renovate our home."

Cory sat quietly for a long moment before taking Sandra's hand. "Can we plant an apple tree in the front yard?"

Sandra pulled her close and kissed her. "Baby, we'll plant an entire orchard of apple trees if that's what you want."

Sandra's first week back in the Dallas office had been a wild series of events. Her announcement that she would be opening a new office in San Antonio and placing Allison in charge of the Dallas office came as a complete shock to everyone but Allison, whom she had spoken with earlier.

Margaret had taken the news much better than Sandra had expected and agreed to move to San Antonio to keep working for her. Then she shyly informed Sandra that Minnie would be moving with her, and was it possible Sandra might be in need of an extraordinary gardener? Sandra agreed that with thirty acres they would certainly need a gardener. Sandra teased her unmercifully until Margaret threatened to cook nothing but tuna casserole for a week. Sandra quickly relented.

Sandra arranged to visit Carol late Thursday afternoon. They met at a restaurant downtown. Carol spent the entire meal talking about her father's impending wedding to Miriam Bell. Miriam's husband had died ten years earlier, leaving her an estate valued at slightly over three million dollars. Carol was sure her father and Miriam would make the perfect couple.

Sandra smiled as she paid the tab. Carol would never change. She handed Carol an envelope containing the deed to the penthouse.

"You always liked the place more than I ever did. You might as well keep it."

"Why are you being so nice to me?" Carol asked as she peeked into the envelope.

Sandra shrugged. "I guess I just want you to be as happy as I am."

"You could live there with me," Carol offered with a small smile.

Sandra shook her head as she stood, kissed Carol's cheek, and wished her the best in life. Carol never asked how Sandra was or where she'd been for the last two months, and Sandra did not bother to tell her.

On Friday, Sandra packed her personal items and shipped them to San Antonio. She left the furniture for Carol. Margaret would be staying with Minnie until the house in San Antonio was completed and Sandra and Cory were ready to move in. Sandra closed the penthouse door for the last time. Turning the key, she smiled. She was finally closing that chapter in her life. She went down the elevator, climbed on her bike and headed for the airport to pick up Cory.

They arrived at Laura's just before five. Laura met them at the door smiling. "I can't believe I'm actually going to meet someone you know," she teased Sandra, hugging her tightly.

Sandra introduced them and Laura gave Cory a hug. "You must be very special to her," she said, studying Cory.

"Let's hope so," Cory said, throwing Sandra a special look.

"Come on in. Dinner will be ready in a few minutes."

"Sandra tells me you're a great cook," Cory said as they made their way to the kitchen.

"She only shows up when she's hungry, so that helps a lot."

Sandra noticed the table was set for four. "Who's joining us."

"Someone I've been seeing. I hope you don't mind."

"You've finally found Mr. Right?" Sandra beamed. "Why haven't you told me?"

"It happened kind of quick. I wanted to be sure before I told you," Laura said and pulled a pan of rolls from the oven. "In fact, I should probably . . ." The roar of a motorcycle sounded from the driveway.

"He rides a bike?" Sandra asked, raising her eyebrows.

"Sandra," Laura said, and began to fidget.

"It's all right. I'm just joking."

The front door opened and footsteps sounded in the hall. "Oh," Sandra teased, looking at Cory. "He just walks right in. Already past the doorbell stage, huh?"

"Leave her alone," Cory scolded.

"Hey, there."

Sandra turned and stared. The kitchen grew deathly quiet.

"Did I come at a bad time?" Dee asked.

"Dee," Sandra managed to gasp. "Dee is, Mr. Right?" She was shouting, but couldn't stop herself.

"I prefer Ms. Right," Dee replied, smiling. "I take it you didn't get around to telling her," Dee said, stepping into the room and kissing Laura.

A swirl of emotions rushed over Sandra. She had not seen Dee since that wild night they had spent together. Plus, there was the fact, Dee herself admitted to being unable to practice monogamy. Sandra felt she should warn Laura. If she stood silently by and Laura got hurt, it would be her fault.

"What happened to your being straight?" Sandra demanded.

"You always told me if the right person came along, anyone could swing either way," Laura reminded her.

Sandra rubbed her face. "Dee, don't do this," she pleaded.

Dee held up her hands. "I know what you're thinking, but I asked her for a commitment." She looked at Laura, and Sandra saw the look of love pass between them.

Sandra felt guilty. What if Laura or Cory ever found out about the night she and Dee had spent together? Sandra looked guiltily from Dee to Cory and then to Laura.

"I know what you're thinking," Laura began, "and I know all about it," Laura assured Sandra.

"How'd you know what's she thinking?" Dee asked puzzled.

"After you've known her for as long I have, you'll know what she's thinking before she does. It's written all over her face."

"So what's she thinking?" Cory asked, raising her eyebrows at Sandra who blushed deeply, causing them all to laugh.

"Dinner is getting cold and we can discuss this later," Laura urged. Sandra sent her a grateful glance. She would tell Cory about Dee, but preferred to do so in private.

After dinner, Cory and Dee insisted on doing the dishes. Sandra and Laura used the time to walk down to where the horses were.

"Are you upset with me?" Laura asked, leaning against the fence.

"Surprised and maybe a little worried, but no, I'm not upset. I want you to be happy. It's just that . . ." She stopped, not sure how to phrase her doubts.

"You're worried Dee is going to love me and leave me," Laura said.

"The Dee I knew was not interested in monogamy."

Laura turned to watch the horses. "Do you plan on staying with Cory for the rest of your life?"

Shocked that she would even ask, Sandra replied firmly, "I love Cory and intend to do my damnedest to make the relationship last. I want to grow old with her."

"Yet you actively participated in a night of lovemaking with Dee with the intent of it only being a one night stand." One of the horses walked up, and Laura rubbed its neck. "If

I had shown any interest the day we kissed in the yard, would you have made love to me?"

"Probably," Sandra answered honestly, a little confused about where the conversation was going.

"Then it's possible to engage in non-monogamous sex with one person and still be able to settle down with someone you love?"

Sandra relented. Laura didn't need her overbearing protection. "I don't know why I hang around you," Sandra said, wrapping her arms around Laura and pulling her back against her.

"Because until a few weeks ago I was the only sane thing in your life, and I never made you eat tuna casserole."

"I give up. You'll never change." Taking Laura's hand, they started back toward the cottage. "So," Sandra started casually, "when Dee comes over to play, does she bring her toys?"

Laura's face turned scarlet, causing Sandra to burst into laughter. Laura grabbed the water hose and Sandra started running. She almost reached the door before the water hit her.

Later that evening, the four women sat on the porch surrounded by the sounds of crickets. Laura and Dee were in the swing; Cory and Sandra were in lawn chairs. Each couple told their story of the past two months and discussed their dreams for the future. In the soft darkness, Cory reached out and took Sandra's hand. At that moment, Sandra realized where her true wealth lay.

About the Author

Frankie J. Jones is the author of *Rhythm Tide, Whispers in the Wind, Captive Heart,* and *Room for Love.* She enjoys fishing, traveling, outdoor photography, and rummaging through flea markets in search of salt and pepper shakers.

Authors love to hear from their readers. You may contact Frankie through Bella Books at BellaBooks@aol.com, or directly at FrankieJJones@aol.com.